To anyone who needs more books like this on their shelves, in their classrooms, and libraries.
Be the change.

Girls to the Front
Copyright © 2025 Niña Mata
Art on page 86 by Lynnor Bontigao.
All rights reserved. Manufactured in Grude, Bosnia and Herzegovina. No part of this book may be used or reproduced in any manner whatsoever without written permission except in the case of brief quotations embodied in critical articles and reviews. For information address HarperCollins Children's Books, a division of HarperCollins Publishers, 195 Broadway, New York, NY 10007.
www.harpercollinschildrens.com
Library of Congress Control Number: 2023940808
ISBN 978-0-06-321628-0
Typography by Kathy H. Lam
24 25 26 27 28   GPS   10 9 8 7 6 5 4 3 2 1
First Edition

# GiRLS to the FRONT

## 40 ASIAN AMERICAN WOMEN WHO BLAZED A TRAIL

WRITTEN AND ILLUSTRATED BY
#1 *New York Times* and Award–winning Illustrator
## NIÑA MATA

HARPER

*An Imprint of HarperCollinsPublishers*

# CONTENTS

I wrote this book for many reasons.

This book is for my daughter and her generation. As a mom I'm always exposing my daughter to stories of women who made giant waves in history just by being themselves and following their hearts. I want to instill in her a confidence that I've only recently found in myself. I want her to know her voice is important, she matters, and that her future is for her—and only her—to decide.

I also wrote this for my younger self. My younger self who constantly felt like a disappointment because I couldn't do math as well as people told me I was supposed to because I am Asian. This is for the girl who would rather write make-believe stories and draw, who felt ashamed that she didn't fit into any of the other Asian stereotypes and didn't know any better to argue against it.

Growing up, history was my least favorite subject. It's said that the purpose of history is to nurture personal identity and to help us learn from our past so we can be our best selves. But most everyone I learned about was a man wearing a funny white wig. I tried with all my might to relate, but the stories never seemed to stick. But what if? What if I had opened a book and it told me an extraordinary story about a girl who looked like me? Would I have always chosen the chair in the back of the class? Or would I have been brave and spoken up when I had something to say? I wrote this because I finally understand the true value of knowing our history and how empowering it could make someone feel about their own purpose.

The idea for this book sprouted during the height of the pandemic, when Asians were being targeted and discriminated against. The news was filled with countless violent acts against people of Asian descent, especially our elders. In March 2021, eight women of Korean descent were killed in a mass shooting in Atlanta, Georgia. Although the incident was not labeled as a hate crime, people spoke up. Stop Asian Hate became a movement, and everyone was getting involved in ways they could. It was at this time that I felt the need to do something.

I took to social media and highlighted one of the victims. With the illustration, I posted a summary of her life and just how full it was. She had a story. She was someone's mother, a daughter, a friend. Her life was worth sharing.

It was also Women's History Month, and I was trying to find inspiration to draw. It dawned on me that there are other Asian women out there I can learn about. So I looked. I wanted to see if I could find women who pushed their way to the front. In my research I found teachers, doctors, artists, scientists, athletes—women who shouted and not only made their way to the front but took center stage! Reading about their stories of bravery, struggle, discrimination, strength, and perseverance changed something in me. These women taught me how to take up space and own it in ways only I can.

When it came to illustrating these women, I drew what I have always loved to draw: portraits. One of my favorite things to draw is faces. Even when I was a kid, I was fascinated by people's faces, especially the eyes. It was, and still is, the very first thing I draw. The eyes are the first thing that I remember about a person; I wanted these portraits to look at us as if they're making eye contact with the reader, because I believe eye contact helps us focus in on the conversation. And I want these conversations to matter.

I hope these women's stories give you the same feeling of empowerment as I have felt. I'm grateful for every one of their journeys, and I admire each one of them because no one ever gave them the opportunities they had—they took them and made a way for themselves. These women are just the beginning. There are plenty more amazing people out there! May these women inspire you and help you on your journey to becoming who you were always meant to be. May this book be a hand waving you to go straight to the front, there's space for you.

Let's *go*!

—Niña Mata

# MARY TAPE

## (1857–1934) • MOM, ACTIVIST

Can you imagine being eleven years old and arriving to a new country all on your own? Mary did just that. She emigrated from China around 1868 and settled in the town of San Francisco. Thanks to her new friends at the Ladies' Protection and Relief Society, she quickly learned English and assimilated into American culture.

Grown-up Mary and her husband, Joseph Tape, were determined to provide a good life for their family and to raise their four children to be upstanding, well-educated Americans. But back in those days, because of the **Chinese Exclusion Act of 1882**, Chinese immigrants were not allowed to become US citizens. Which meant that, despite modeling upstanding American behavior, the Tapes, because they were Chinese, didn't have the same rights as their friends.

Mary wanted the same privileges for her children as her neighbors had. She wanted her kids to go to the same school their friends were in. But the only schools available for Chinese Americans were missionary schools in Chinatown. So when Mary's daughter Mamie was denied an education at the nearby public school, Mary put her foot down. Mary sued the school and San Francisco's Board of Education. She said in an open letter to the board, "Is it a disgrace to be born a Chinese? Didn't God make us all!!! What right have you to bar my children out of the school because she is [of Chinese descent]?"

Mary was right, and the California Supreme Court agreed with her, citing that not only were the Tapes paying taxes that supported the public school but it was also against the **Fourteenth Amendment** to deprive any child "equal access to education regardless of ancestry." In 1885, Mary and the Tapes won the case *Tape v. Hurley*.

Although Mamie Tape would never attend the primary school, San Francisco saw more and more Chinese Americans attending historically public white schools after her case. Mary and Mamie's case was one that inspired the landmark case of **Brown v. Board of Education of Topeka**—seventy years later!

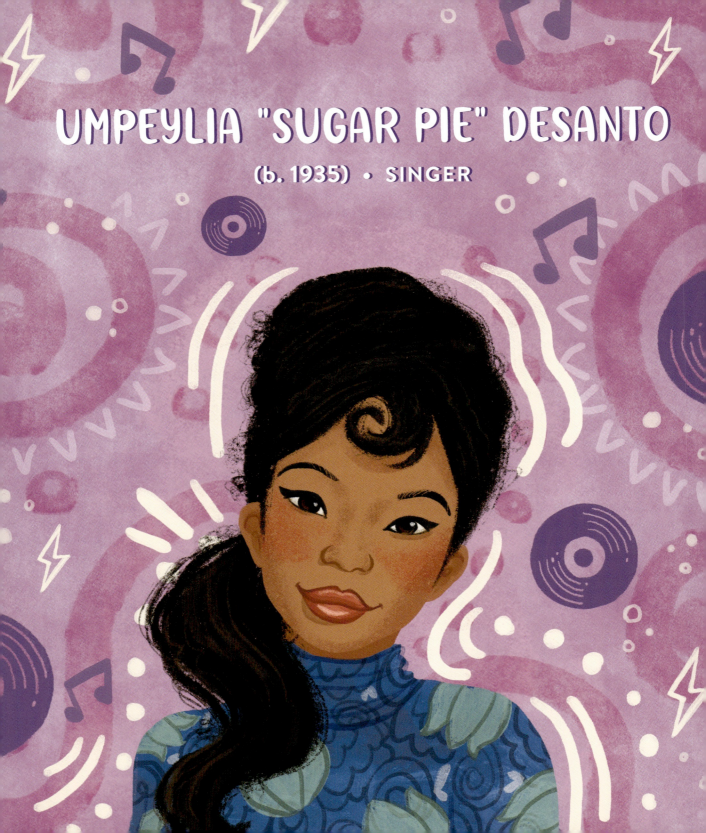

# UMPEYLIA "SUGAR PIE" DESANTO

## (b. 1935) • SINGER

Umpeylia Marsema Balinton grew up in a diverse neighborhood in San Francisco. So being Black and Filipino was never an issue for her; she was friends with kids of every race. Umpeylia and her friends loved music. Forming a girl group called Lucky 20's, Umpeylia and groupmate Henrietta (Etta) James would hang out by their porch and harmonize.

One day, Umpeylia entered a talent show at her local theater. Her powerful voice carried throughout the hall as she sang the blues. And as if that weren't impressive enough, she sang barefoot onstage because she would do backflips as she performed. She won the talent show that night. Umpeylia kept entering competitions and would win each and every time. She won so much that the organizers asked her to stop competing. That's when she decided it was time to enter other competitions.

When Umpeylia competed at a show in Los Angeles, she met Johnny Otis, who was known as the "Godfather of Rhythm and Blues." Johnny was so blown away by Umpeylia that he offered her a contract and gave her the stage name "Sugar Pie." Sugar Pie went on to tour with the legendary R&B singer James Brown. She has had many hit songs, including a duet with her friend Etta James called "In the Basement." Sugar Pie also recorded "I Want to Know," produced by Bob Geddins Sr., the Godfather of Oakland Blues. The song rose to number 3 on the *Billboard* charts, and Sugar Pie signed a record deal with Chess Records. Chess Records included artists like Etta James, Chuck Berry, Muddy Waters, Buddy Guy, and Bo Diddley. During her tenure at Chess Records, Sugar Pie was the highest paid writer in their company, with a songbook containing more than one hundred compositions.

In 2005, at the age of seventy, she released her latest album, called *Refined Sugar*, proving that passion and raw talent know no boundaries. In 2008, Sugar Pie was awarded the Pioneer Award by the Rhythm & Blues Foundation for her significant contributions to the music. Sugar Pie kept winning, even without trying.

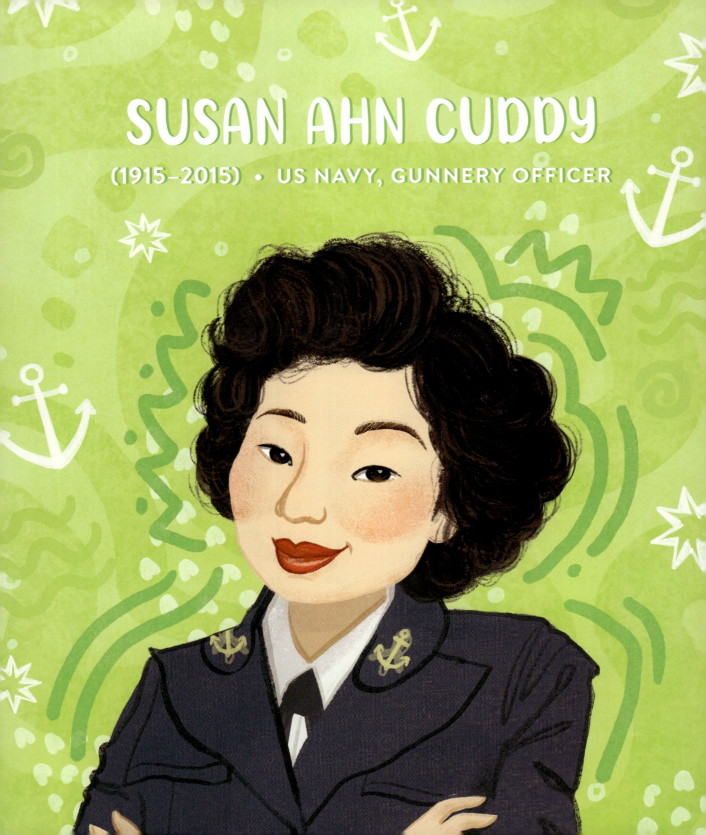

# SUSAN AHN CUDDY

## (1915–2015) • US NAVY, GUNNERY OFFICER

Susan's dad was her hero. He was one of the leaders of the Korean Independence Movement and resisted oppressive Japanese rule. As conditions worsened, Susan's pro-independence parents fled Korea to the United States before she was born. In 1932, Susan's dad traveled to China for a mission and was captured by Japanese military. Her dad was tortured for years and eventually died in captivity.

By the time World War II began, the fight against Japan became personal for Susan. If US victory meant Korean independence from Japan, she was determined to help fight the war any way she could. When she first enlisted in the US Navy, they turned her away because she looked too much like the enemy. Susan was raised to be persistent, and she kept trying.

One year later, during the height of the war, Susan tried enlisting again, and this time they accepted her in the US Navy. Susan was part of the first group of WAVES (Women Accepted for Volunteer Emergency Services). Her commanding officers recognized her talent for teaching while she was assisting an aerial gunnery instructor, and Susan became the first woman gunnery officer in the US Navy. Her job was to teach fighter pilots how to shoot down enemy aircraft.

One day during training, she was confronted by a disobedient soldier who disliked taking orders from a woman, especially one of Asian descent. She looked straight at him and told him she didn't care what he thought of her. "You shoot when I tell you to shoot," she said. Despite all her hard work and efforts, Susan dealt with a lot of racism and sexism throughout her service. But it never stopped her from doing what she believed was fair. Susan was eventually promoted to lieutenant.

After the war, she became an intelligence officer working to decipher codes for the navy. And in 2003, Susan was named Woman of the Year by the State Assembly of California for her dedication to public service. Susan's dad might have been her hero, but her service to this country makes her one of America's heroines.

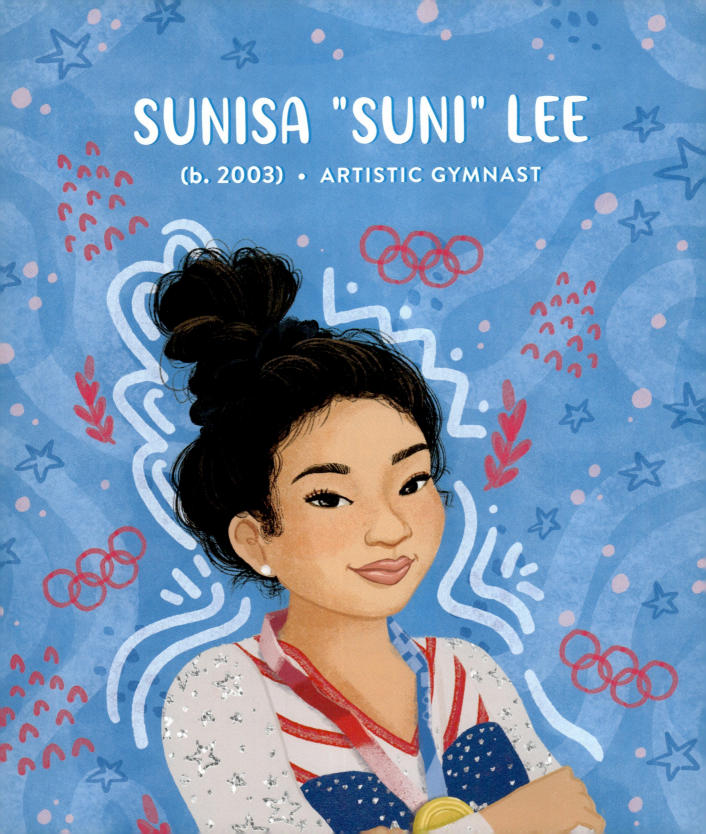

# SUNISA "SUNI" LEE

## (b. 2003) • ARTISTIC GYMNAST

**G**rowing up in Saint Paul, Minnesota, Suni was a super active kid. She loved flipping and tumbling around everywhere so much that her parents signed her up for gymnastics class at six years old. Her parents couldn't afford to buy a balance beam, so her dad made her one from some wood and an old mattress.

Suni worked twice as hard because training at six years old was considered late for a gymnast. In between gymnastics classes, she would practice on her makeshift beam and her dad would always be there to cheer her on. Eight-year-old Suni was improving at a quick pace, moving up three gymnast levels in a span of one year! At eleven years old, she reached the highest level one can achieve in the **Junior Olympics program** and qualified to train as an Elite gymnast. Only 2 percent of gymnasts compete in this level, and Suni earned her spot in just a few years of training.

Two days before the 2019 national championships, Suni's dad was helping a friend trim a tree. He fell off a ladder, causing him to be paralyzed from the chest down. Suni wanted to quit and stay in the hospital to help take care of her father, who was due for surgery. Knowing how hard she'd worked for this moment, her dad persuaded her to stay in the game. The day of the national championship, with no family around, she took a deep breath, found her focus, and set out to have fun, as her dad advised. Suni won the silver in all-around competition and was one routine closer to her Olympic dreams.

On July 29, 2021, at the Tokyo Olympics, Suni became the first Asian American woman to win the Olympic gold in the individual all-around competition and won gold at the Paris Olympics in 2024, bringing so much pride to her Hmong heritage and, especially, to her family.

From spinning on *Dancing with the Stars* to being named one of *TIME* magazine's one hundred most influential people in the world, Suni continues to raise the bar.

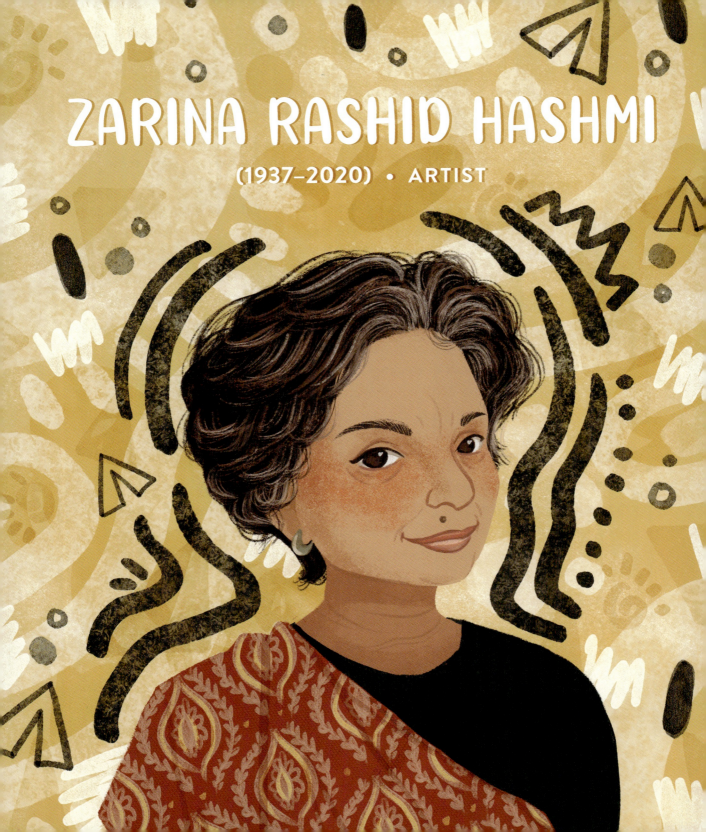

# ZARINA RASHID HASHMI

## (1937–2020) • ARTIST

Zarina Rashid Hashmi was born in India. She had a big family. On hot summer nights, she and her sisters loved sleeping outdoors, where they would plan and imagine their limitless future.

In 1947, violence and chaos broke out between two religious groups in her country: Muslims and Hindus. This historic time is now called the **Partition of India**. To avoid the conflict, like millions of Indians of all faiths, Zarina and her family fled their home to a refugee camp. Home would never look or feel the same again after that day. In the camps, she saw a lot of grief, death, separation, and fear. The emotions that swirled around this experience weighed heavily on her. Zarina carried these feelings with her throughout her whole life.

Years later, she would marry young diplomat Saad Hashmi. They traveled the world together because of Saad's job. It was their trip to Bangkok that sparked Zarina's interest in printmaking. She loved experimenting with textures and color. She played with all types of medium and scraps of wood. This passion for creating led to more experiments with wood carving.

When Zarina's husband passed away, she moved to New York City. She joined the feminist art movement, gaining a passion for the city and its beautiful community. In the 1980s, Zarina, alongside Cuban artist Ana Mendieta and Japanese artist Kazuko Miyamoto, organized an exhibition of women artists from developing nations called *Dialects of Isolation* at the A.I.R. Gallery in New York City. She received many awards and had her artwork shown in some of the most famous museums around the globe.

Associated with the minimalist movement, Zarina's work is known for her use of geometric and abstract shapes and textures. Sometimes she would even include calligraphic text in Urdu. Having lived many places throughout her life and having her first home taken away from her, Zarina's work centered around her search for "home." Zarina was able to take the pain from her childhood and repurpose it into symbolic safe houses for anyone who has ever felt displaced and far away from their haven.

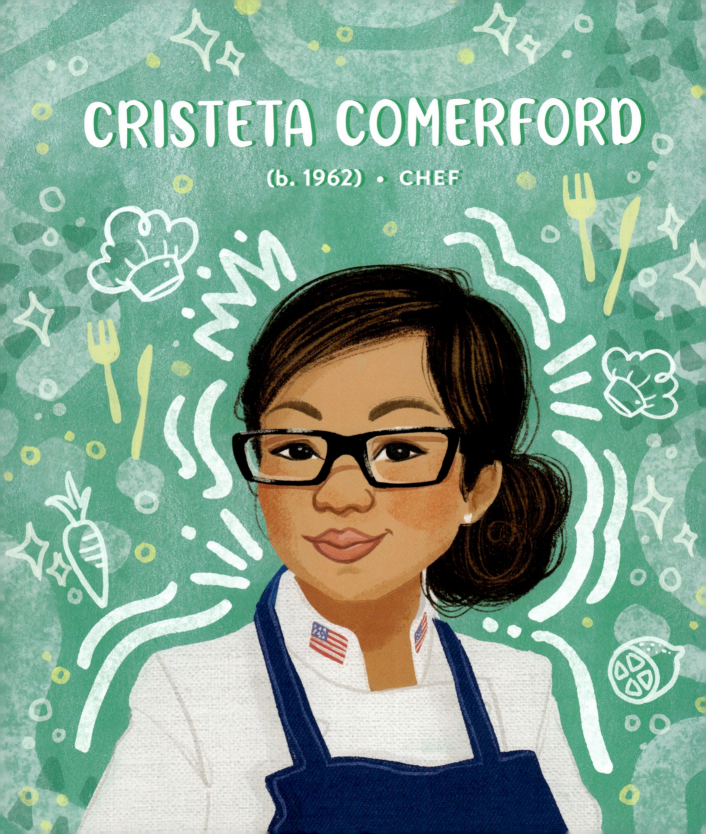

# CRISTETA COMERFORD

## (b. 1962) • CHEF

As a child, Cristeta loved going to her grandma's house in the outskirts of Manila, Philippines. "Everything was right in their backyard," she said. Her grandparents had rice paddies and chickens and a garden of vegetables. They ate what they grew. She enjoyed the smells of her family's cooking. She would play and experiment with different flavors throughout her childhood so much that she studied food technology at the University of the Philippines.

In 1985, at the age of twenty-three, Cristeta immigrated to the United States to pursue a culinary career. She worked in hotel kitchens and studied for six months in Vienna, Austria, before being recruited by White House executive chef Walter Scheib III. She worked for the Clinton administration in the 1990s. When it was time for Chef Scheib III to retire, Cristeta jumped at the chance to apply for the position of executive chef of the White House. Out of 450 applicants across the United States, Cristeta was offered the job.

In 2009, Michelle Obama, First Lady of the United States, had an idea. She wanted to start a garden for the White House for all generations after to enjoy. Cristeta was thrilled and more than happy to help. It reminded her of her grandma's garden all those years ago. She loved the inviting way a garden brings people together and fosters a sense of family, which Cristeta knew and cherished.

She once mentioned that because she is proud of her heritage, some of the meals she would prepare for the White House had a touch of Filipino influence, such as adding adobo flavors to the stuffing. Cristeta is the first woman, first person of color, and, specifically, the first Asian (Filipino) American executive chef of the White House. Cristeta hung up her apron after serving five administrations, and she will *always* be remembered for throwing down in the White House kitchen!

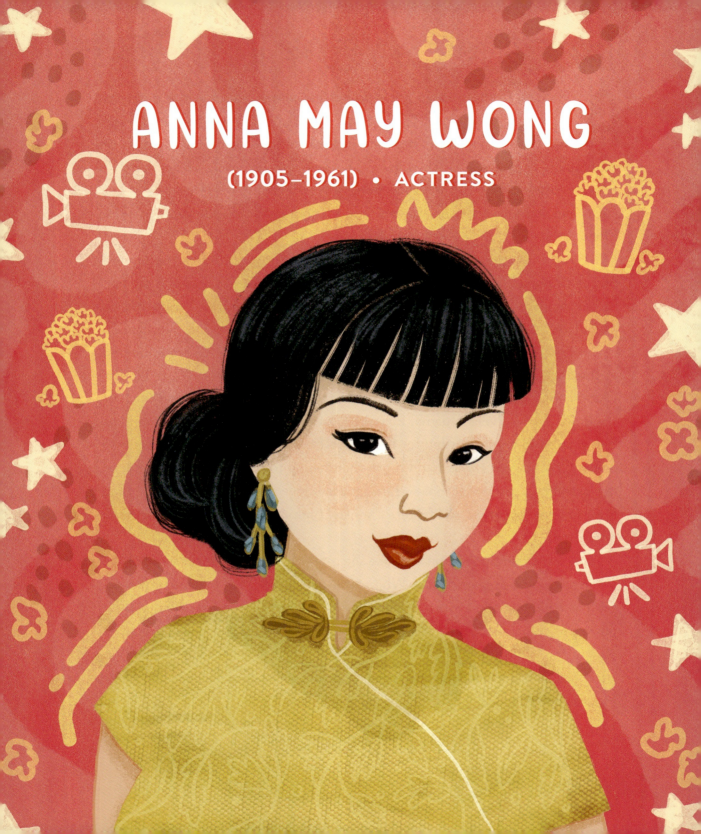

# ANNA MAY WONG

(1905–1961) • ACTRESS

Anna May Wong, born Wong Liu Tsong, was raised in California and felt more American than Chinese. But growing up as a first-generation Asian American kid during the early 1900s, Anna was constantly reminded that she was "too American" for her Chinese peers and "too Chinese" for her American peers. Movies were her way to escape from being bullied for looking different. Instead of going to school, she spent her lunch money to watch movies at **Nickelodeon theaters**. That's how Anna fell in love with the art of cinema. She dreamed of becoming a movie star.

By the time she was seventeen, Anna landed her first starring role in a movie called *The Toll of the Sea*. She received rave reviews for her acting chops and was even known to steal the scene from her costars. Anna May had star power! Although Anna obviously had enough talent to play the lead, she was often given the part of the vixen, a concubine, or the villain, which was how Asian women were portrayed in movies. Lead roles meant for Asian Americans were given to white actors who performed in **yellow face**, wearing heavy makeup that reshaped their facial features.

Despite the constant prejudice Anna faced, she kept on making movies. She traveled to Europe in search of better roles and even starred in an operetta in Germany. Although she had a successful career in Europe, she eventually came back home to the United States. Anna starred in over fifty films, including *Piccadilly*, *Shanghai Express*, and *Daughter of the Dragon*, and even had her own TV show. She spoke up about the lack of diversity in the roles she and other Asians were (and are) allowed to play in Hollywood and about equal pay for women.

Anna May Wong is considered the first Asian American movie star, recognized as one of the four trailblazing "Ladies of Hollywood," which includes actresses Dorothy Dandridge, Dolores del Rio, and Mae West. Because of her accomplishments, Anna was added to a US quarter in 2022, making her the first Asian American ever honored on American currency.

After all these years, Anna still knows how to make a scene!

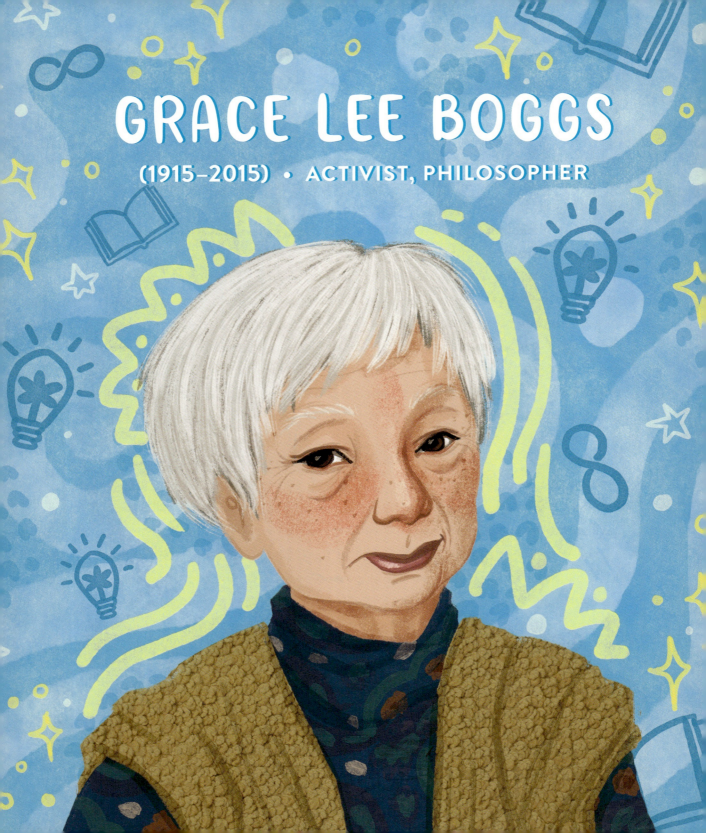

# GRACE LEE BOGGS

(1915–2015) • ACTIVIST, PHILOSOPHER

When Grace got her PhD in philosophy in 1940, she knew exactly what she wanted to do: teach. But no one would hire her as a professor because she was first-generation Chinese American and a woman. To get in academia, she became a librarian at the University of Chicago instead. The job paid ten dollars an hour and included housing in a rat-infested basement on the South Side of Chicago.

Due to the great migration from the South, more than sixty thousand Black people moved to Chicago in search of better jobs. But when people got to the city, they were pushed to the South Side, also known as the **Black Belt**, and lived under terrible living conditions. One day while walking around her neighborhood, Grace saw Black residents protesting. Grace dealt with more than her fair share of racism and sympathized with the struggle. No one deserved to live a lesser life because of the color of their skin or the shape of their eyes. Grace decided to join her neighbors and rallied to expand tenants' rights. This began her commitment to fight racial injustice.

A few years later, Grace moved to Detroit, where she became a notable figure in Detroit's Black Power movement. She also became editor of the radical newsletter *Correspondence,* where she met another activist named James "Jimmy" Boggs. Sharing the same values, they married in 1953. Together, Grace and James were part of nearly every major social movement. Grace organized the March to Freedom of 1963 in Detroit, where Dr. Martin Luther King Jr. gave a version of his "I Have a Dream" speech. She also organized the Grassroots Leadership Conference of 1963 where Malcolm X gave his well-known "Message to the Grassroots" speech.

When Grace wasn't in front of the line fighting for what she believed in, she was writing about it. Grace authored five books about her philosophy on being a solutionary and social activism: *if you see a problem in your community, work together to fix it!* She might have lived a life of struggle and discrimination, but she handled it all with grit and grace.

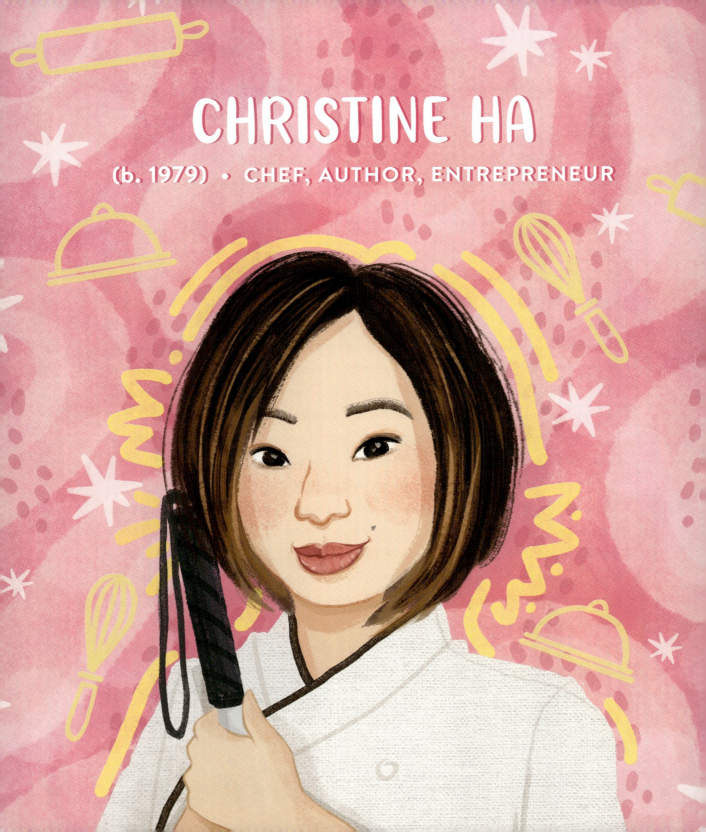

# CHRISTINE HA

**(b. 1979)** • CHEF, AUTHOR, ENTREPRENEUR

Christine always wanted to help her mom in the kitchen. She thought her mom made the best dishes from their native land of Vietnam. Although her mom considered it too dangerous for Christine to help with the cooking, her mom would sometimes let her mix the filling for the egg rolls.

In college, Christine pursued a degree in business until she started feeling sick. The doctors couldn't figure out the cause of her paralysis and other symptoms. Eventually, Christine was diagnosed with neuromyelitis optica (NMOSD), which is an autoimmune disease that causes vision loss. Christine became legally blind at age twenty-eight.

Being visually impaired caused Christine to reexamine her life. She went back to school and got a master's degree in creative writing. After living in a dorm, eating frozen pizzas and ramen regularly, Christine craved her mom's Vietnamese home cooking. But her late mother never got the chance to pass down her recipes. So, when Christine moved into her first apartment, she was determined to re-create dishes from her childhood. She was seeing only large blurry shapes at the time—but that didn't stop her. Christine just had to relearn her way around the kitchen. She started using technology like a talking scale and thermometers to help her cook.

Christine combined her new passion for cooking and her love of writing and created a successful blog called *The Blind Cook*. In 2012, she competed on the third season of **MasterChef**. Christine was the first blind contestant to ever compete on the show—and she won! She was awarded $250,000 and a cookbook deal. Her first cookbook, *Recipes from My Home Kitchen*, was an instant bestseller in 2013.

Winning *MasterChef* allowed Christine to expand her business and bring attention to NMOSD. Since then, she has opened two successful restaurants, the Blind Goat and Xin Chao. Christine has also partnered with NMOSD advocacy groups and launched initiatives to raise awareness and encourage anyone with the disease that they are "very much capable."

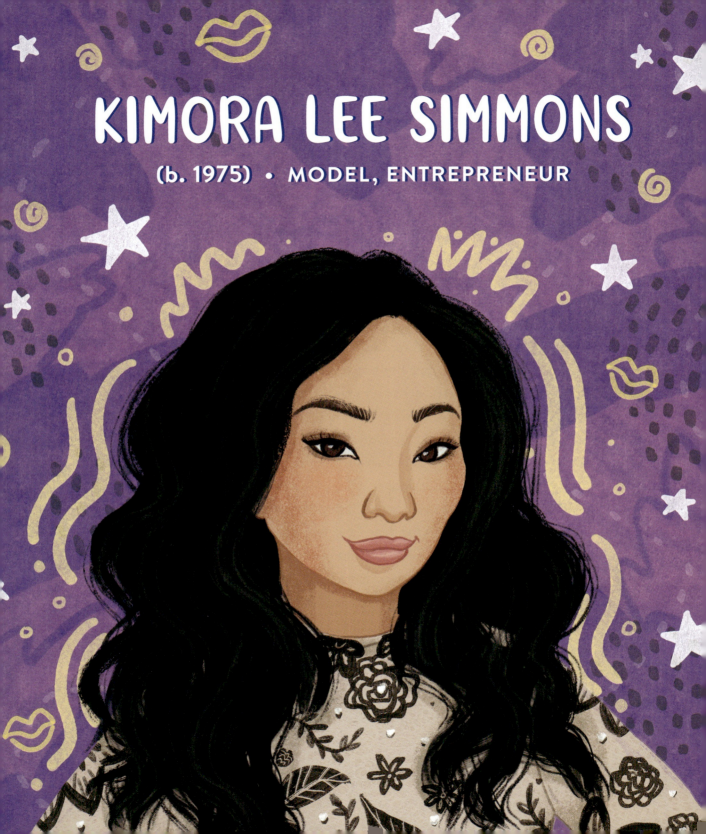

With a mother of Korean and Japanese descent and a father who was African American, Kimora Lee Simmons found life as a biracial kid hard. Kids would tease her all the time because she was tall and she had her mother's eyes and the mixed hair texture of her parents. When Kimora was ten years old, she was so tall kids at school would call her names like "Chinky giraffe." She didn't fit in anywhere, and her mom noticed how it was affecting her confidence.

When Kimora turned eleven, her mom signed her up for modeling school. "Put on your game face," she would tell Kimora. She wanted Kimora to see that her unique features were beautiful. Kimora felt comfortable in front of the camera and on the runway. Those were the only places she could be herself and where her features stood out in a good way.

At thirteen years old, Kimora signed with a modeling agency and was sent to Paris. She was hired by Karl Lagerfeld, who was the head fashion designer of Chanel at the time. Kimora became Karl Lagerfeld's muse; he called her the "Face of the Twenty-First Century." In 1989, Kimora closed out Chanel's **haute couture** show, which, at the time, was one of the most iconic jobs on a runway. She inspired Karl's vision, which opened the door to more inclusion and diversity within the industry. This would launch Kimora's successful career in fashion, as she continued modeling for elite designers of the industry like Fendi, Valentino, and more.

Since then, she has become a philanthropist, fashion icon, business mogul, and television personality. Kimora is considered one of the first Asian American fashion designers after launching her label Baby Phat in the early 2000s. Baby Phat became a successful women's clothing brand with its iconic velour tracksuits. In 2020, she relaunched Baby Phat to include a beauty line, which is led by her daughters, Ming and Aoki Lee Simmons.

Kimora took the term *mogul* to new and inspiring heights.

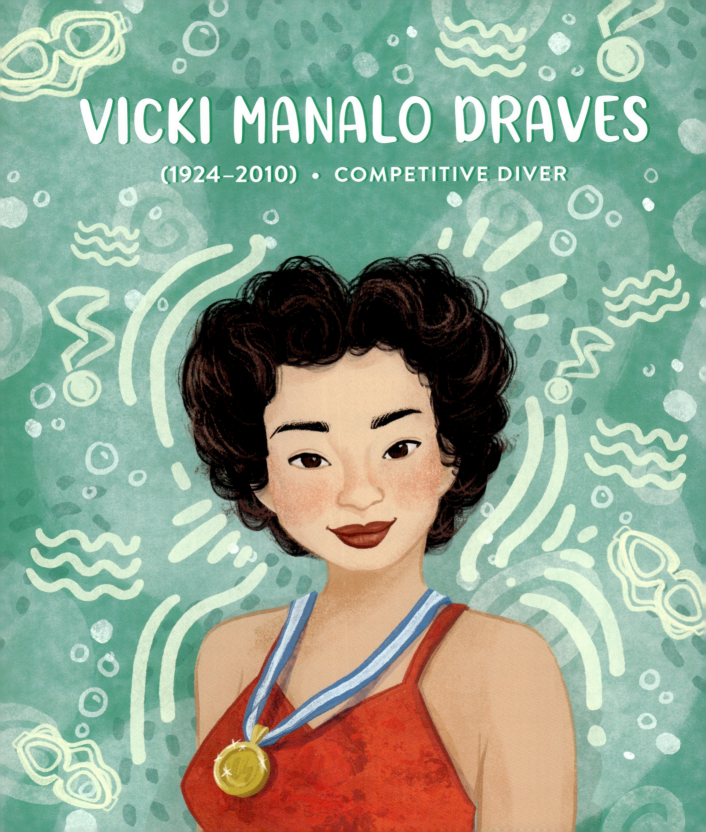

Vicki Manalo dreamed of becoming a ballerina. Even though her parents couldn't afford ballet lessons, that didn't stop her from being active. She loved sports like badminton, basketball, and softball. One hot summer day, Vicki and her twin sister decided to go to the local pool in the Mission District of San Francisco. This is where she discovered her love of diving. She would practice as much as she could and as often as possible.

Vicki lived in the 1940s, and back then, all public pools were still segregated and mostly for whites only. Since Vicki was half Filipino, she, like all people of color at the time, was allowed to swim in the pool only once a month, right before the pool would be drained. Vicki loved diving so much, a diving coach took notice of her fearless form. But because of the residual prejudice against Asian Americans after World War II, Vicki wasn't allowed to practice in the private pools or to compete. As suggested by her coach, she took her English mother's last name, Taylor, and continued diving competitively.

When Vicki was nineteen, she met her future coach and husband, Lyle Draves. Lyle helped improve her diving style. Lyle insisted that she needed to start fresh and act as if she'd never had a diving lesson in her life. With her new coach and a new way of looking at diving, Vicki won five United States diving championships. In 1948, Vicki won two gold medals at the Summer Olympics in London, becoming the first Asian American woman to win a gold medal and was inducted into the International Swimming Hall of Fame in 1969. Although Vicki once confessed in an interview that she "was really kind of afraid of water," she dived right in and faced it.

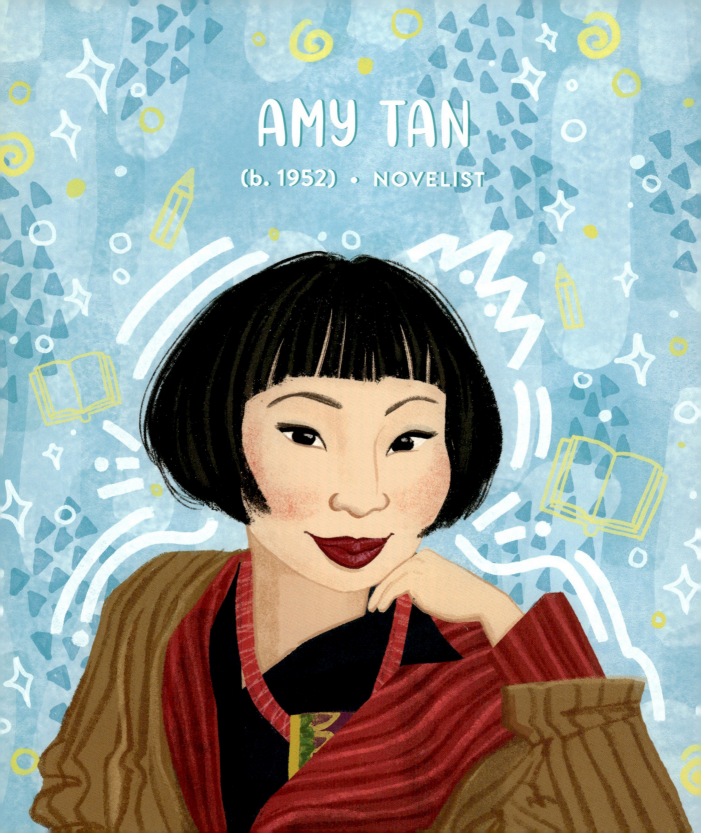

# AMY TAN

(b. 1952) · NOVELIST

Growing up in Oakland, California, Amy Tan knew that her parents had reasons for fleeing China and taking refuge in America. She loves her family, but Amy had a complicated relationship with her mother. She always assumed it was because they grew up in two different worlds and cultures. Her relationship with her mother would be further strained when Amy told her she wanted to be a writer.

Amy became a freelance writer, working ninety hours a week writing speeches for technological companies. It wasn't exactly her dream job, but she was determined to prove to herself she could make a living with her words. During her downtime, Amy wrote stories. She began writing short stories loosely based on her childhood and the people in her life. Amy discovered that writing about her experiences became a therapeutic way of exploring her relationship with her mother and a way of preserving her mother's memories.

Amy's agent, Sandra Dijkstra, saw something special in these stories. She saw a novel in the making after combining Amy's short stories together. Sandra pitched the idea to the biggest publishing houses in New York. Everyone wanted to publish it. The book started a bidding war between publishers, and it was sold for $50,000. That type of offer was unheard of at the time, as it was rare for publishers to gamble with a debut author.

Amy finished writing *The Joy Luck Club* in four months, and her book was released in 1989. Since then, it has sold millions of copies, won multiple literary awards, and has been adapted into a full feature movie starring an all–Asian American cast. The success of this book opened the doors for many first-time writers. She went on to publish over a dozen critically acclaimed books, including the children's Sagwa series, starting with *The Chinese Siamese Cat*.

All Amy set out to do was explore her relationship with her mother. Her ability to be vulnerable and honest in her writing created space for an otherwise invisible culture to finally be seen.

# DR. CHIEN-SHIUNG WU

**(1912–1997) • SCIENTIST**

D r. Chien-Shiung Wu's love for science started at an early age when her dad, an engineer, opened the first all-girls school in China. Over time, this interest in math and science became a passion, and Chien-Shiung would move to America to get her PhD in nuclear science at the University of California, Berkeley.

After getting married in 1942, she was offered a teaching position at Princeton, which was still an all-male school at the time, making her the first ever female instructor of the Department of Physics. Dr. Wu's time at Princeton was cut short when she was invited to join the super top secret Manhattan Project to develop the first atomic bomb during World War II. When the war ended, she went back to teaching, this time at Columbia University. After speaking up for herself regarding equal pay, Dr. Wu was paid just as much as her male colleagues.

In 1956, Dr. Wu's colleague at Columbia University Dr. Tsung Dao Lee and his friend Dr. Chen Ning Yang were conducting an experiment that disproved the law of conservation of parity did not apply to beta decay of nuclei. The two scientists were having trouble and asked Dr. Wu to help. And she did! Dr. Wu conducted the experiment that proved Dr. Lee and Dr. Yang's hypothesis. This was huge for the world of physics! This discovery earned Dr. Lee and Dr. Yang a **Nobel Prize** but not Dr. Wu. Even though Dr. Wu's experiment was what led to the breakthrough discovery, she never got credit for it likely because she was a woman in a predominantly male field.

But that didn't stop her from being one gnarly scientist. Though she would never be awarded the Nobel Prize, Dr. Wu kept doing what she loved. She continued to teach science at Columbia, conduct experiments, and win many accolades thereafter. Dr. Wu structured her life full of elements and compounds that mattered to her, and she shared that energy with the world.

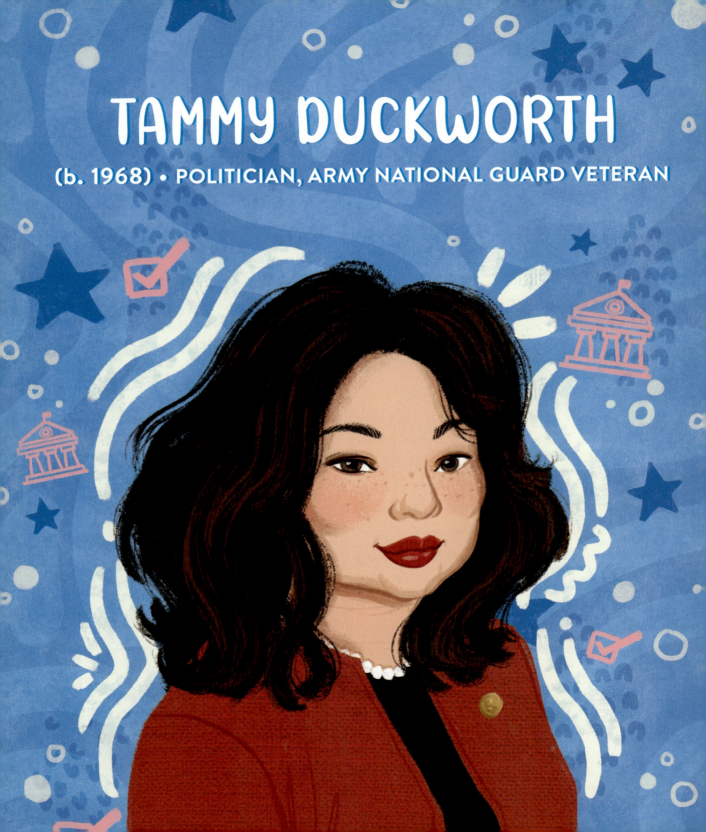

# TAMMY DUCKWORTH

(b. 1968) • POLITICIAN, ARMY NATIONAL GUARD VETERAN

When Tammy Duckworth joined the army, she was determined to become a helicopter pilot. In the 1990s, it was one of the few combat jobs a woman could pursue. Tammy was the only woman in her helicopter training class, and she aced it. During **Reserve Officers' Training Corps (ROTC)**, she also met her future husband, Bryan Bowlsbey. When her training ended, they moved to Illinois, and she went back to school. Tammy was still serving in the reserve forces while she pursued a PhD in political science. In the middle of the fall semester, she was deployed to Iraq.

In 2004, Tammy was called in to fly a BLACK HAWK helicopter in the Iraq War. It was post 9/11, and the situation was very tense in Iraq. The military bases were attacked daily. On November 12, 2004, during a routine mission, Tammy's helicopter was struck down by a rocket-propelled grenade. Luckily, she survived but had lost both her legs.

Because she experienced firsthand how important good health care coverage was to a veteran, she vowed to make sure veterans would get the benefits and care they deserved. She became the director of the Illinois Department of Veterans' Affairs and was later appointed assistant secretary of veterans by President Barack Obama. In 2012, Tammy became the first Asian American and first disabled woman to ever be elected to the US House of Representatives.

In 2016, she became the first disabled woman to hold a seat in the US Senate. When Tammy announced she was expecting her second child, in 2018, she became the first woman to give birth while holding office.

Days after giving birth, Tammy was expected to be back at work to vote. But children weren't allowed on the Senate floor. Tammy pushed to allow babies to accompany their parents while in office. The rule was passed, and the next day, Tammy and her week-old baby, who was properly dressed in a blazer, went to vote. Proving once again that women can literally do it all!

# LUCY LIU

(b. 1968) • ACTRESS, ARTIST, ADVOCATE

Lucy Liu is a critically acclaimed actress and director. She has starred in many films, including the early 2000s *Charlie's Angels* franchise and the pop culture classic *Kill Bill*, and directed episodes on television series like *Elementary*. In 2019, Lucy was honored with her very own star on the Hollywood Walk of Fame in California. And even as her accolades as an actress continue to grow, Lucy still pursues one of her first passions: art. From ink drawings, collages, and paintings, the emotional, evoking art Lucy creates touches you and makes you think.

She grew up in Queens, New York, with Chinese immigrant parents who worked all day. Most of the time, Lucy and her siblings would have to take care of themselves. This included walking to and from school on their own. Lucy loved collecting random objects she would find on her walks around the neighborhood, such as old pens, soda can tabs, and even hubcaps. She would bring the discarded items home because she felt bad for them and wanted to offer them a safe place.

This hobby of collecting random objects led to an art series called "Lost and Found," which was a collection of sculptures, like books whose pages have been carved out to make holes to house the discarded objects she'd found on the streets. Lucy said the series was about finding a place to belong and the feeling of being cared for. A lot of Lucy's underlying themes in her art are about being protected and finding a home.

Her works have been featured and displayed all around the world, including at **Art Basel** in Miami, Florida, and at a 2019 exhibition called *Unhomed Belongings* at the National Museum of Singapore. Because she is also an ambassador for **UNICEF**, Lucy donates a lot of her profits from her art shows and art books to the organization. Lucy is truly a Renaissance woman. There is nothing she cannot do.

# GYO FUJIKAWA

## (1908–1998) • ILLUSTRATOR

Gyo Fujikawa was born and raised in California in an all-white neighborhood, and because of her ethnicity she never felt like she fit in. Gyo would often draw as an escape. One day, her teacher noticed how good she was at drawing and helped Gyo get into Chouinard Art Institute. After graduating, Gyo was one of the only female illustrators hired by Walt Disney Studios in 1939.

This was around the same time tensions grew between Japan and the United States at the brink of World War II. Following her work on *Fantasia* in 1941, Disney sent her to their advertising department in New York City, which helped her evade being sent to **Japanese American internment camps**. Since her family was sent to the camps, she often felt guilty she escaped. Gyo was ashamed to be Japanese and hid her identity until Walt Disney himself asked why she was hiding when she was an American citizen with the same rights as everyone else.

In 1957, Gyo was asked to illustrate a children's book called *A Child's Garden of Verses* by Robert Louis Stevenson. The book became a success and catapulted her career in children's publishing. Gyo loved drawing kids being kids.

When Gyo decided to write and illustrate her first children's book, *Babies*, she wanted to draw babies of all skin colors, races, and ethnicities. Her publisher worried the book would not do well if she were to add Black and Brown children in it. Gyo insisted that the book be as inclusive as possible, as that's how she saw the world. The book was a hit. It became a bestseller!

Throughout Gyo's career, she created over fifty children's books. Her work has been translated into seventeen languages and published in twenty-two countries. She became one of the first illustrators to ever include racial diversity in children's books. A game changer in her industry, she was also one of the first illustrators to get royalties for her work. Thanks to Gyo and many illustrators who followed in her footsteps, books are a great window of this colorful world.

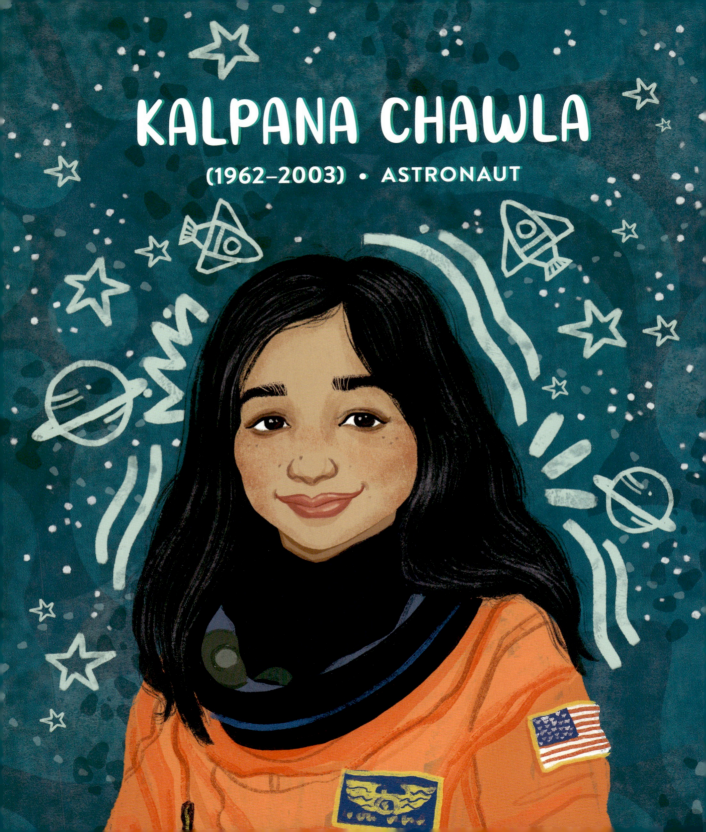

# KALPANA CHAWLA

## (1962–2003) • ASTRONAUT

Kalpana Mantu ("one who imagines" in Hindi) Chawla had many hobbies; she loved hiking, reading, and looking up at the stars. But what she loved the most was watching airplanes take off with her dad at a local flying club in India. The day she learned about astronauts flying above and beyond the sky, Kalpana knew she wanted to go to space one day. Even though education in India in the 1970s was scarce for a girl like Kalpana, with the support of her parents, she was able to go to school. During recess, she would make paper airplanes and watch them fly.

Kalpana took her love of flying and how planes were built and majored in aeronautical engineering—that's when her love for aircrafts and space grew. After graduating, Kalpana moved to Texas to study space engineering. When she finally finished school, she got her dream job at NASA. There, Kalpana implemented new ways of looking at things; she made groundbreaking discoveries in aerodynamics and presented innovative ideas that scientists are still using today.

One day, Kalpana was selected to become an astronaut candidate for a space mission to orbit the Earth. She studied and trained for over a year. Out of the handful who applied, she passed with flying colors. The very next year, Kalpana was up in space living her dream as an astronaut. She logged more than thirty days in space. Kalpana and her team did all kinds of fun experiments, like studying the sun as close as humanly possible!

Kalpana was the first South Asian American woman to ever become an astronaut and fly to space. She blazed a path for so many young female scientists. She even started a program to inspire the next generation of scientists by sponsoring two students from her school in India to visit the NASA facilities, encouraging everyone to reach beyond the stars.

# HELEN ZIA

**(b. 1952)** • ACTIVIST, JOURNALIST, AUTHOR

A daughter of Chinese immigrants, Helen Zia was often told to go back to where she came from. But Helen was born and raised in New Jersey. For all she knew, she was exactly where she was supposed to be. Helen wished that she had someone to help her stand up to bullies who told her otherwise. She grew up during the height of the civil rights movement, and she admired people like Dr. Martin Luther King Jr., Rosa Parks, and Malcolm X, who spoke out against injustice—and bullies.

In the 1980s, after graduating from Princeton, Helen got a factory job in Detroit while trying to figure out what to do with her life. The work conditions were treacherous, and Helen wondered why no one was talking about the conditions in the news. Feeling frustrated and inspired, Helen got to know her coworkers and wrote the story herself. This began Helen's career in journalism. Most important, this drove her passion to share stories about people that would otherwise not be heard.

A year before joining the Detroit *Metro Times* as associate editor, Helen saw a small news clipping about a Chinese American named Vincent Chin, who was killed by two white men. Although the men denied it, most people saw this as a racially motivated crime. The two men were charged with manslaughter, for which they'd only pay a fine.

Helen and Vincent Chin's mother, Lily, fought and spoke out against the verdict. Helen reached out to everyone she knew, especially the activists she worked with for other social causes. Everyone came to help. Justice for Vincent would be one of the first times Asian Americans formed a united front, spearheading an organized Asian American movement. Helen's activism would inspire future generations to stand up to hate crimes and for equal rights for all.

Helen continues to advocate and agitate through her writing. The author of award-winning books like *Last Boat Out of Shanghai* and *Asian American Dreams*, she uses her voice to fight for civil, women's, and LGBTQ+ rights. She pushes back against bullies everywhere!

**B**efore Ny Sou was born, her parents lived in Cambodia during the rise of the **Khmer Rouge regime**. The regime was a violent and bloody system of government in Cambodia's history. Its dictator, Pol Pot, took over the Cambodian government in 1975, and gave orders to kill anyone who didn't agree with his political views. Thousands of people died during this genocide.

When Ny Sou's parents realized that their family was in danger, they snuck away on bicycles, carrying only what they could, which was their children. They biked and walked approximately eighty miles from their home and sought temporary refuge when they reached the Vietnam border.

After a few years, they decided to go back home to Cambodia. It was then that Ny Sou was born. They returned hoping things had gotten better. But the country was still turbulent and unsafe. The family had no choice but to keep going. So they packed up their things once again and headed to a refugee camp in Thailand. Then they filed for asylum in three countries, including the United States. Months later, their application to America was granted. Her family settled in Long Beach, California. Ny Sou's family worked hard and struggled at times to adapt to the culture, but they remained grateful for their new home and opportunity for peace.

Ny Sou excelled in school and loved every subject, including science. She went on to become a mechanical engineer at NASA and helped create the head of the famous **Mars Perseverance rover**, a car-size robot that looks for ancient signs of life on Mars and rock samples that can be brought back to Earth to study. Ny Sou and her family watched a livestream of the rover launch into space from the comfort of their home in 2020.

From one journey of finding refuge to another journey seeking life on Mars, Ny Sou knows very well the value and rewards of persevering.

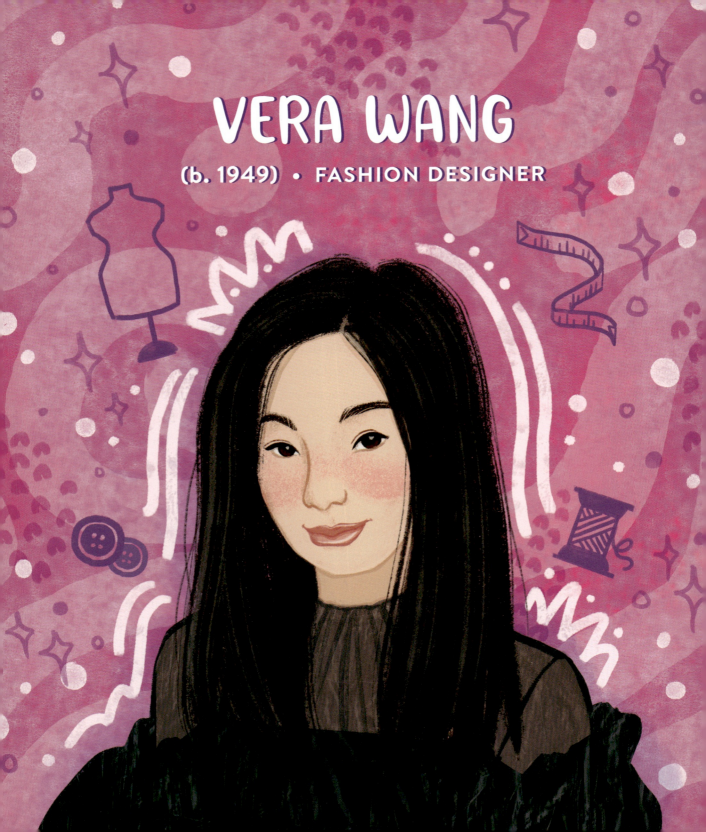

# VERA WANG

## (b. 1949) • FASHION DESIGNER

Growing up in New York City, Vera Wang had only one dream. She wanted to be an Olympic figure skater. She started skating at the age of seven and trained hard, determined to make it to the Olympics. But as hard as she tried, she still couldn't qualify. As much as Vera loved figure skating, she made a very hard and painful decision to hang up her skates.

After college, Vera pivoted to fashion and started working for *Vogue* magazine, becoming one of the youngest editors of the time. She worked for *Vogue* for seventeen years, until she decided to switch gears again and became a design director for Ralph Lauren.

By the time she was forty, she fell in love and got engaged. Vera hadn't realized that choosing a wedding dress would be the hardest part of getting married. None of the dresses she saw aligned with who she was. Some dresses were too traditional, too lacy, too plain, or too "out there." She saw herself in a less traditional, more modern dress. She had a clear vision of what she wanted to wear in her head, so Vera designed it herself. This would spark her idea of creating contemporary wedding dresses for other women. In 1990, Vera opened her own wedding boutique, which launched one of the most iconic fashion labels in the world.

Vera's signature style has since expanded to television, books, and retail. And although she is best known for her iconic wedding gowns and high fashion, she also designed figure skating dresses for some of the top Olympic athletes of our time.

In 1992, Vera was asked to design a costume for figure skater Nancy Kerrigan. Figure skating dresses were known to be bold and heavy. Vera went in a different direction. She designed a dress that would not only look stunning but also be light enough to help Nancy land those difficult jumps. During the 1992 Winter Olympics, Nancy Kerrigan glided across the rink in a crowd-pleasing white dress that stood out for its simplicity.

It looks like Vera made it to the Olympics after all.

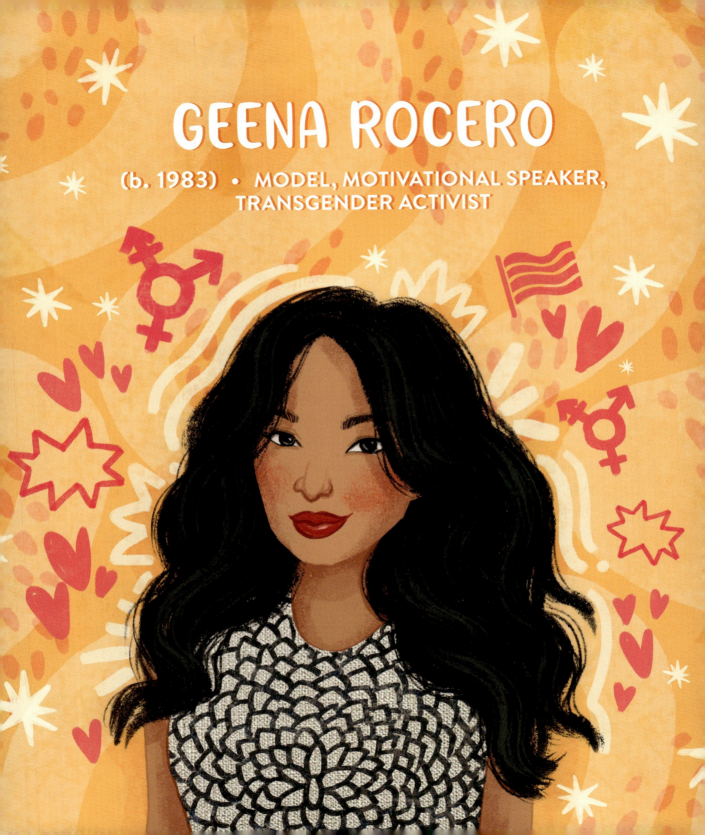

# GEENA ROCERO

(b. 1983) • MODEL, MOTIVATIONAL SPEAKER, TRANSGENDER ACTIVIST

**I**dentity is a pretty hard word to define at a young age, but Geena always knew who she was. Geena was born and raised in the Philippines, and although assigned male at birth, she was free to be herself in the comforts of her home. She loved playing with Barbie dolls and dressing up. Her family loved her for who she was, and Geena felt empowered by it.

Unfortunately, the outside world was not as loving or accepting. When Geena would dress and act how she felt, some people would make fun of her, saying mean and scary things. But this never swayed how she felt on the inside. Geena competed in and won many beauty pageants in her town. Competitors would call her a "horse," but her trans mother helped Geena reclaim the term—reminding her that she's elegant and has "mythical energy." She had become a pageant celebrity.

Although pageants helped affirm her identity, the one thing that Geena had always wanted was a driver's license with her correct gender on the card. This could not be done in the Philippines. Geena decided to move to San Francisco. While other people her age were excited to get their driver's license to enjoy the freedom of driving, for Geena her driver's license meant something more important. Having her gender on her license was an affirmation of who she was. She was a woman.

In 2005, Geena moved to New York City to pursue a career in modeling, and within months she became one of the most sought-after fashion models. Still, for years, she was too afraid to reveal her true story. Then, in 2014, she gave a moving keynote at a TED conference, where she came out as a transgender woman to everyone for the first time. She received a standing ovation, and the talk has been viewed over six million times. Geena is currently a successful supermodel, a transgender advocate, and founder of Gender Proud, a media production company dedicated to telling transgender stories much like hers. The rest is *her*story.

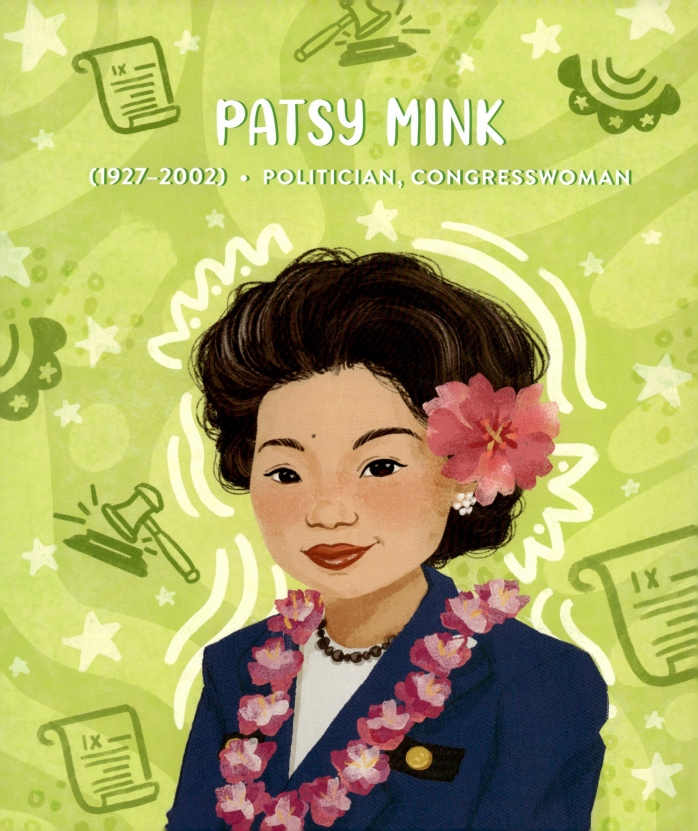

# PATSY MINK

## (1927–2002) · POLITICIAN, CONGRESSWOMAN

Patsy heard "No, you can't" all her life.

Her childhood dream was to be a doctor. When she was in medical school in Nebraska, she wanted to be in the same dormitory as her friend, and the school said, "No, you can't." Because of the school's housing policy, Patsy was placed in a segregated dorm where foreign students and American students of color were housed. She was outraged. So Patsy went around the school community gathering support to abolish the policy. And the very same year, the administration dismissed the rule.

After graduating from medical school, Patsy applied to be a doctor in hospitals around the United States and was rejected because she was a woman. By now, Patsy was down but not out. She decided to change career directions and go to law school. ("What, like it's hard?") She earned her law degree, passed the bar, and applied to several law firms—only to face the *same* discrimination. No one would hire her as a lawyer because she was a woman. So she decided to start her own law firm—the first in Hawaii led by a woman. It was Patsy's law career that opened her eyes to the fact that if you want something changed, you've got to make the change yourself.

Patsy wanted to run for the House of Representatives for Hawaii. The Democratic Party told her, "No, you can't." They didn't think that a Japanese American would ever win votes, especially right after World War II. Patsy didn't care. She went around the neighborhood, canvassing—knocking on people's doors and telling them why she would make a good candidate.

In 1964, Patsy won a seat in the House. She became the first woman of color to be elected to the United States Congress and served six terms in the House of Representatives. Patsy helped write many laws, especially ones that affected women and education, like **Title IX**, the **Early Childhood Education Act**, and the **Women's Educational Equity Act**.

So, while the whole world screamed, "No, you can't," all Patsy listened to was that voice in her saying "Yes, I can."

# GABRIELLA WILSON (H.E.R.)

## (b. 1997) • SINGER, SONGWRITER, ACTRESS

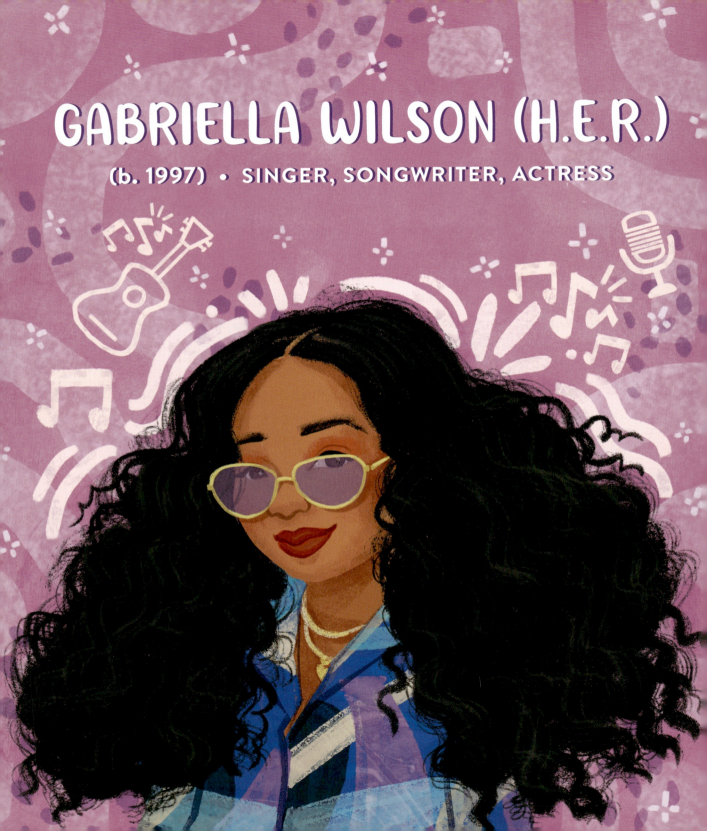

Gabriella "Gabi" Wilson grew up surrounded by music. From listening to jazz and funk while her parents made breakfast, to watching her father and his band rehearse in their living room, music was always playing in her house. When her dad's band took breaks, they would let Gabi take the mic to practice her singing. Young Gabi kept a diary where she'd write down her feelings, sometimes in rhyme, which would turn into songs. By the time she was ten, Gabi had already performed at the Apollo Theater in New York City and was singing for the *TODAY* show. These opportunities introduced her to very important people in the music industry. By fourteen, she was offered a record deal. But Gabi still took the time to allow herself space to grow.

At sixteen, Gabi knew how to play several instruments and was writing and creating her own songs. These songs were rooted in her personal experiences and raw emotions. So, when she shared some of her songs with the rest of the world, Gabi wanted to remain as anonymous as possible, hoping the work would stand on its own. She went under the pseudonym H.E.R., which stands for "having everything revealed."

When Gabi released her **EP**, *H.E.R. Volume 1*, it got the attention of many new fans, including artists such as Alicia Keys, Usher, Drake, and Rihanna. Gabi kept her identity from the public because she knew her songs spoke to everyone. She didn't want people to put labels on who she was. Pretty soon the music industry had H.E.R. on the top of their hit lists and everyone wanted to know who H.E.R. was.

Since her first breakthrough EP, Gabi has performed many sold-out tours and has won Grammy Awards and an Academy Award. She even played princess Belle for ABC's *Beauty and the Beast: A 30th Celebration*, where she gave a grand finale with her signature sunglasses on and guitar in hand. These days, everyone knows Gabi's name!

# DR. ERIKA LEE

## (b. 1970) • HISTORIAN, PROFESSOR, AUTHOR

Erika Lee studies history from the ground up. She was raised in San Francisco and received her PhD from the University of California, Berkeley. During her college years, she became curious about her family's history and immigration story. She began to dig and found that her roots in America stem seven generations deep.

The first person in her family to immigrate from China came around 1854, during the **California gold rush**. Erika learned about the discrimination and injustices her ancestors dealt with at the time (see "Chinese Exclusion Act of 1882" in the glossary). She quickly realized these stories were similar for most Asians in American history. Asian people were considered unworthy, and white Americans felt that giving Asian people any rights would "endanger the very essence of the United States."

For Erika, this hit home when she discovered her great-grandfather was detained at the **Angel Island Immigration Station** for two weeks upon arriving in America. To avoid deportation, her great-grandfather paid a thousand dollars to get new papers that changed his identity as a merchant's son. He had to answer over 140 questions about his "on-paper life" and "on-paper family" correctly in order to be released from Angel Island.

The Chinese Exclusion Act was eventually abolished in 1943, but for many Asian American families, the trauma they endured is forever embedded in their history, reminding other generations of their sacrifices. By the time Erika graduated from college, she became passionate about weaving these stories and experiences into the tapestry that is American history, as well as tying them to current issues.

Since then, she has been awarded and recognized as one of the nation's leading Asian American historians, penning four award-winning books. In 2020, she won the American Book Award for *America for Americans: A History of Xenophobia in the United States*. Erika was given the Andrew Carnegie Fellowship (also called the "Brainy Award"). Erika is currently a history professor at Harvard University, still helping to fill in the gaps of American history.

When Chloe was four years old, her father was exploring different hobbies, so he took the whole family snowboarding. While her parents went snowboarding for the experience, Chloe came away with a newfound interest. She genuinely enjoyed snowboarding and loved gliding down the slopes. It was something that just felt natural for her.

At age six, Chloe entered a local snowboarding competition, and she won third place. Chloe thought it was cool that she had won a bronze medal and she hadn't even practiced. Chloe imagined what she would accomplish if she started to practice—like for real. So, after school, her parents would drive her up to the mountain and train. A few years later, she started snowboarding competitively and winning.

When she was eight years old, she moved with her aunt to Switzerland so she could learn French and use her free time to train in the Alps. By the time she was thirteen years old, and back in California, she was competing in the **X Games**. Chloe won a silver medal in the SuperPipe competition, making Chloe the youngest competitor to ever earn a medal at the games. Now she's a six-time X Games gold medalist!

Although she was clearly ready and qualified to compete in the 2014 Winter Olympics, Chloe was way too young to enter. So she waited. In between the waiting, she just kept practicing. Then at the age of seventeen, in the 2018 Winter Olympics—held in South Korea, where her parents emigrated from—Chloe became the first and youngest woman to compete in snowboarding and win gold in the Winter Olympics.

In 2021, she took a short break from the slopes to attend Princeton University. She competed again in the Beijing Winter Olympics in 2022 to become the first female two-time gold medalist in the snowboard halfpipe competition. Some would even say she's the snowboarding GOAT—just ask Olympic Games fans!

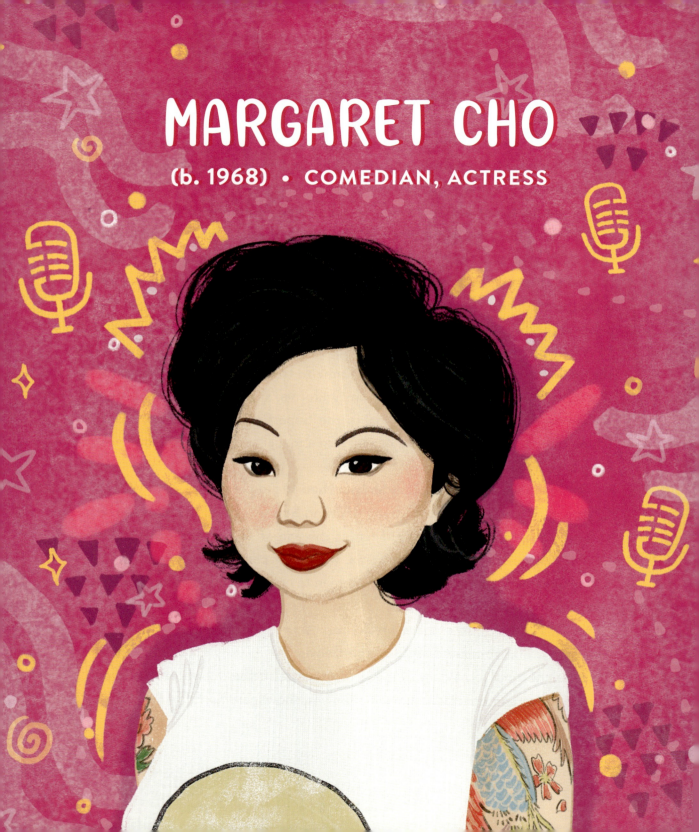

# MARGARET CHO

(b. 1968) • COMEDIAN, ACTRESS

**M**ost people of color have experienced or will probably experience some form of racism in their lifetime. Some have been teased for the shape of their eyes, the color of their skin, the texture of their hair; for Margaret, racism showed itself in how unseen she has always felt.

Margaret Cho's parents emigrated from Korea to the United States in the 1960s. Like many new immigrants, Margaret's parents were in survival mode. They worked hard to adapt to their new country. Most of the time, Margaret's babysitter was their television. When she was seven years old and growing up in San Francisco, she always gravitated toward watching comedy. She loved watching Flip Wilson, Richard Pryor, and Joan Rivers create a career out of making people laugh. From the moment she realized she could make a living out of comedy, she was committed to writing jokes. Margaret started doing stand-up at the age of sixteen, and by the time she was in her twenties, she had gotten so good onstage that she was given the opportunity to tour with fellow comedian Jerry Seinfeld.

In the 1990s, there was an ongoing trend to give comedians their own sit-coms, and in 1995, Margaret Cho was offered to star in her very own. The show was called *All-American Girl*, a prime-time sitcom that starred an all–Asian American cast for the first time ever. Although the show lasted just one season, the show continues to be a major stepping stone for Asian American representation in television history. In 1999, in Margaret's critically acclaimed one-woman comedy show, *I'm the One That I Want*, she discusses the struggles she faced with her television show and with Hollywood in general.

Margaret continues to do stand-up comedy and uses her platform to advocate for LGBTQ+ rights. She is often referred to as the Patron Saint of Outsiders, vowing to make sure everyone feels seen and heard.

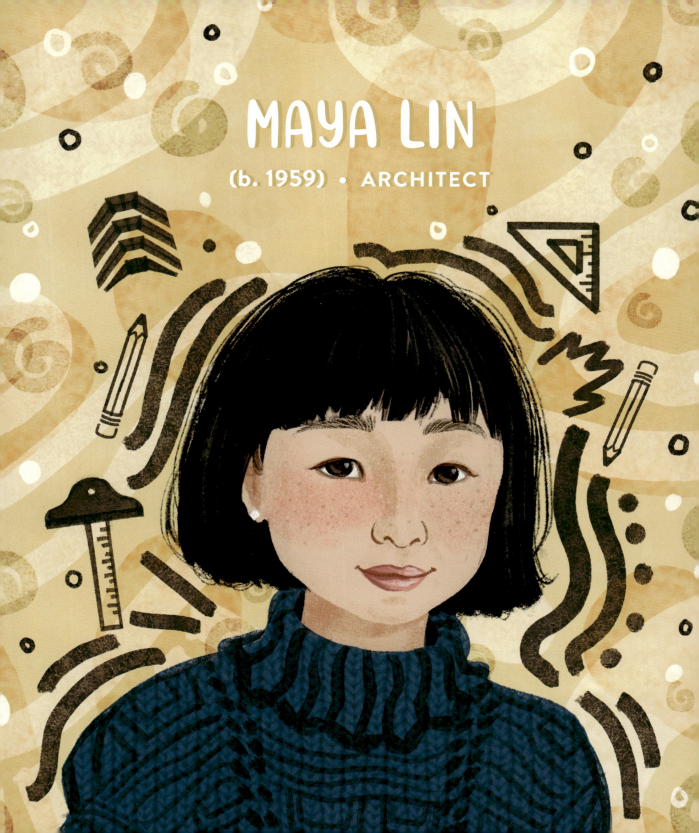

The year was 1980. The Vietnam War was over but not forgotten. To commemorate the fifty-eight thousand fallen US soldiers, the Vietnam Veterans Memorial Fund wanted to build a memorial in Washington, DC. They held a nationwide contest, and everyone was invited to participate. Twenty-one-year-old architect major Maya Lin was a senior when her class at Yale University turned this nationwide competition into a class project.

Maya Lin's vision of two black walls parallel to each other, which met at the end to make a V shape, was something she really thought long and hard over. She wanted to create a memorial that would start from the earth and be so tall that it seemed to reach the sky. The black walls would have every fallen veteran's name inscribed on them to remind the world of their sacrifices. The tips of the V-shaped memorial would point to the Lincoln and Washington Memorials. Maya's teacher was so blown away by her design that she entered the piece into the real competition anonymously. There were over 1,420 submissions, and the judges announced that Maya Lin had won and they would be building her memorial design.

When some people found out she was the architect, they started protesting against the monument, citing that Maya was too modern, inexperienced, and looked too much like the "enemy" to ever be associated with this memorial. Even though this dispute divided some people, the monument was built. It stands tall and proud for anyone who comes and see. Today, the Vietnam Veterans Memorial is one of the most visited memorials in Washington, DC. In a study done in 2010, this memorial has been known to help Vietnam veterans cope with PTSD just by visiting the walls.

Maya Lin is currently a world-renowned sculptor and architect. She continues to design and build some of the country's most recognizable structures, including the Civil Rights Memorial in Montgomery, Alabama, and the 9/11 Memorial in New York City, and consistently proves that there is more than meets the eye.

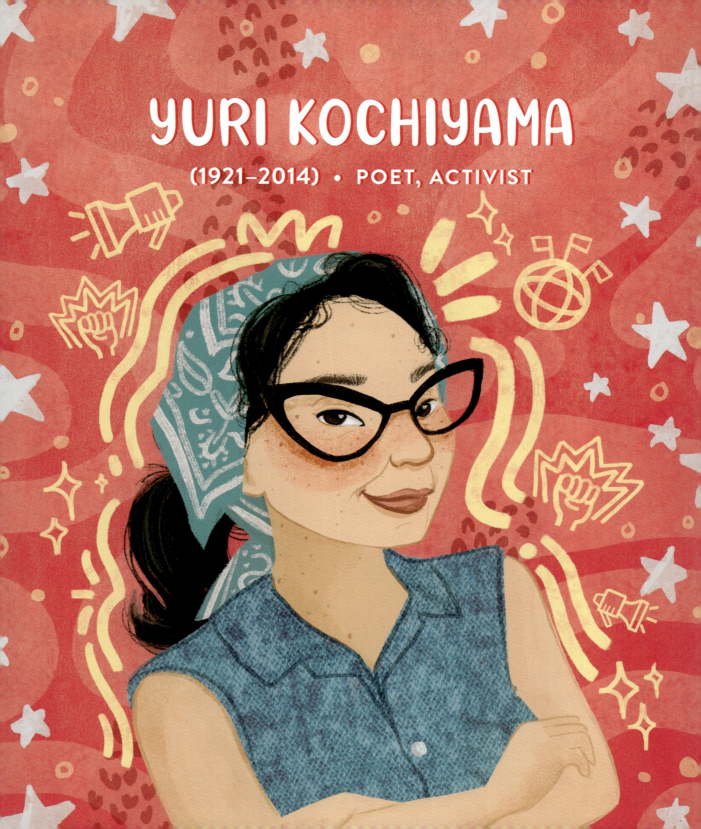

Yuri was your typical all-American Cali girl. She loved playing sports, reading poetry, and volunteering for the Girls Scouts. She described herself growing up "red, white, and blue" and never having experienced racism as a kid.

After Japan attacked **Pearl Harbor** in 1941, things started to change for Yuri. The neighbors would avoid her family. Her church canceled the Sunday school class she was teaching. And in 1942, Yuri's family and thousands of other Japanese Americans were sent to internment camps in Arkansas by order of President Franklin D. Roosevelt. Although Yuri identified as American, she suddenly felt alienated from everything she thought she knew. Suddenly the only country Yuri had ever called home no longer felt safe. Three years later, after her and her family's release, Yuri realized just how much her country needed to change.

In her early forties, Yuri and her husband, Bill Kochiyama, moved to Harlem, New York. They became heavily involved with the racial justice movements and befriended another activist named Malcolm X. Yuri and Malcolm shared similar points of view and spoke out against social issues like racism, nuclear weapons, and the Vietnam War. They became good friends and wrote each other frequently. They even shared the same birthday! When Malcolm was tragically shot in 1965, Yuri knew she had to continue the work.

Yuri believed in solidarity, so her activism spanned a variety of social issues across various groups. She helped draw attention to Puerto Rico's struggle for independence and fought to free many political prisoners, like Black Panther member Mumia Abu-Jamal. In the 1980s, Yuri joined the redress and reparations movement for Japanese Americans who had been placed in internment camps during World War II. She demanded reparations for everyone who was forced to live in the camps and endured the senseless trauma. The government heard her and humbly righted their wrong. After 9/11, Yuri fought against racial profiling of Arabs, Muslims, and South Asians.

Yuri grew up believing she was all-American, and now many Americans will grow up knowing that her dedication to social change was for all.

# KRISTI YAMAGUCHI

## (b. 1971) • FIGURE SKATER

**K**risti was born with club feet, a foot condition that causes feet to point inward. She was forced to walk with a cast and foot braces at a very young age. As she got older, the doctors prescribed her with corrective shoes and encouraged hobbies that would help straighten her feet. Her doctors thought skating was a great idea.

Kristi fell in love with the sport. She practiced six days a week for five hours a day. She felt a different type of confidence on the ice. The way Kristi would get lost in the music and glide across the rink made her feel free. By the time she was in junior high, she was competing nationally and won many awards, including the singles event at the World Junior championship. Then, in the winter of 1992, Kristi won a gold medal for America in the Olympics in the women's singles in France—making her the first Asian American to do so. She did what no one else could since Dorothy Hamill, one of Kristi's biggest idols, had won it in 1976.

In 1992, Kristi continued to dazzle in skates on the "Stars on Ice" tour, which donated their profits to the Make-A-Wish Foundation. Because she comes from a community-oriented family, her years on tour inspired Kristi to pursue her passion in philanthropy. In 1996, Kristi launched the "Always Dream Foundation" to help low-income families and their children. The foundation provides educational and literacy programs, giving thousands of families better access to books every year.

Kristi continues to inspire future generations to follow their dreams. She was inducted into the US Figure Skating Hall of Fame (1998) and the World Figure Skating Museum and Hall of Fame (1999). She is also the author of bestselling children's books like *Dream Big, Little Pig*, and in 2024 Mattel honored Kristi with her very own Barbie! Kristi's enduring perseverance led her to an amazing career with her feet—the star of the show and always guiding her onward.

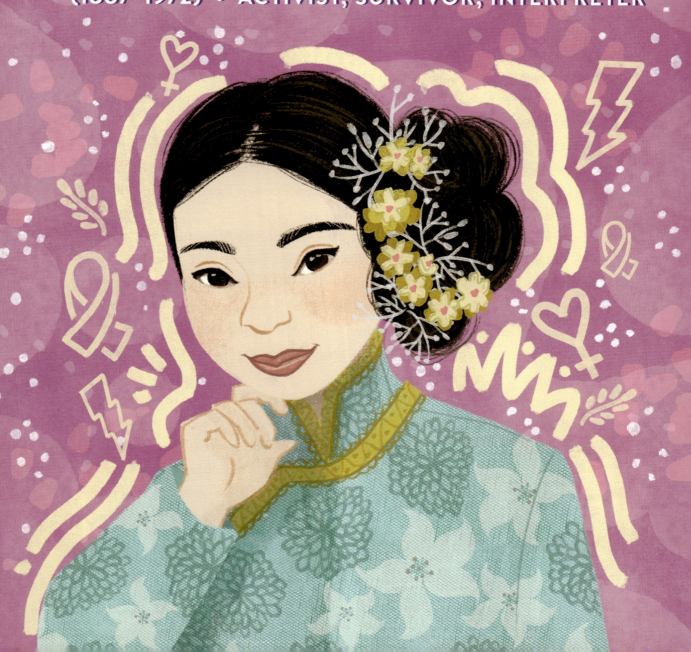

# TYE LEUNG SCHULZE

**(1887–1972)** • ACTIVIST, SURVIVOR, INTERPRETER

Tye Leung always valued her freedom of choice. But by the time she was eleven years old, her mother tried to sell her off to domestic servitude (not once, but twice). Although this arrangement was not uncommon, Tye refused and ran away from home. She found refuge in a missionary school in the heart of San Francisco's Chinatown, which was run by a sewing teacher and activist named Donaldina Cameron. Donaldina's mission was to end sex trafficking, especially among newly immigrated Chinese women, also known as the **yellow slave trade**.

Tye knew firsthand how it felt to be forced into something, so she did everything she could to help the missionary's cause. Tye became an interpreter for women who escaped brothels and helped free about three thousand women. But she didn't stop there.

By the time she was twenty-four, Tye became an interpreter for Angel Island, in San Francisco Bay, where they "processed" thousands of Chinese immigrants coming into the United States. Being the first Chinese American woman to work for the US federal government, Tye did not take her responsibilities lightly. Her role as interpreter came in handy for incoming immigrants who were arriving in a country that didn't really welcome them there (see "Chinese Exclusion Act of 1882" in the glossary). She was known to be kind and understanding and gave them a sense of comfort, as many immigrants were often interrogated and detained for weeks and even months at a time.

Tye knew how unfair these governing rules against Chinese people were and knew she could make a difference just by exercising her freedom of choice. In 1912, eight months after women in California were given the right to vote, Tye was first in line for the ballot box. She voted! A right she utilized nine years *before* the **Nineteenth Amendment** changed the game for all American women. Tye became the first Chinese American woman to ever vote in a US election. That translates as a win for all of us.

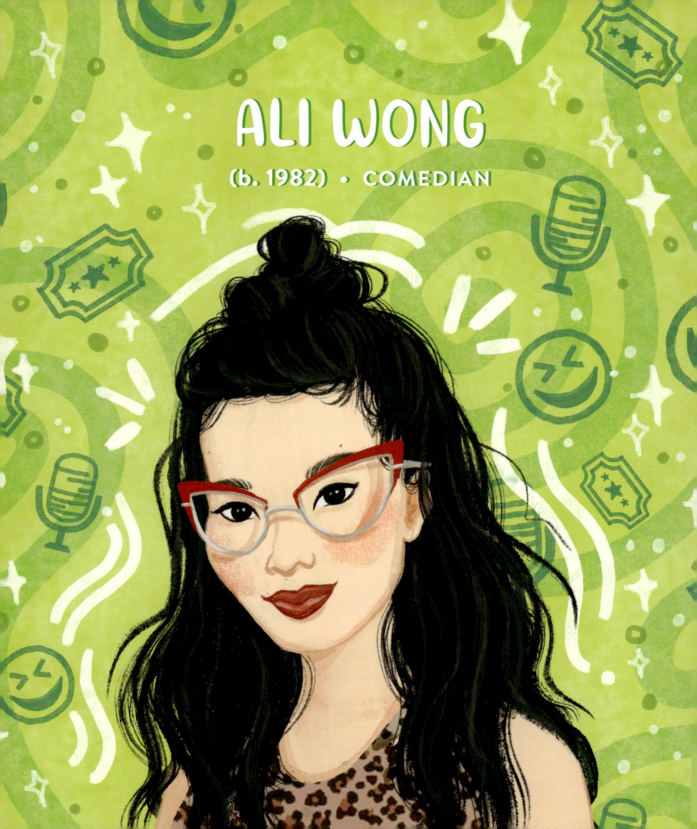

When Ali Wong first stepped into the world of stand-up comedy, her fellow comedians, who were predominantly men, told her she was "cute but too raunchy." They suggested she tone down her work. Some people didn't feel comfortable hearing explicit jokes about the female anatomy; they didn't want a woman's point of view on sexuality or intimacy.

But Ali was raised to speak her mind. She wanted to stay true to who she was. Besides, Ali didn't understand why none of her male counterparts—who were just as vulgar—were advised to clean up their acts. As an Asian American woman, she often found herself working harder than her peers to be respected in the male-dominated industry. When she lived in New York, she would work hard perfecting her craft so much that she would perform nine sets a night, jumping from one venue to another.

Ali continued to make headway in her career by appearing on late-night talk shows and doing guest appearances on television. In 2014, she became a staff writer for *Fresh Off the Boat*, a sitcom starring an all–Asian American family. Then, in 2016, she released her first Netflix special, *Baby Cobra*, a taping of a live stand-up show she performed while seven months pregnant with her first child. Ali would later do a second stand-up special, *Hard Knock Wife*, which was performed while seven months pregnant with her second child. Both specials did really well and were critically acclaimed shows. Ali's ability to joke about the pains of motherhood, marriage, and her honest search for work-life balance makes her stand out from the crowd. She's not afraid to speak her truth.

In 2018, Ali wrote her first book, *Dear Girls*, as an autobiographical letter to her two daughters and all-round life guide. It was inspired by a letter from her father she received after he passed away. *Dear Girls* became an instant *New York Times* bestseller. Ali won her first Golden Globe in 2024, making her the first Asian American woman to win in her category.

All the funny girls, stand up!

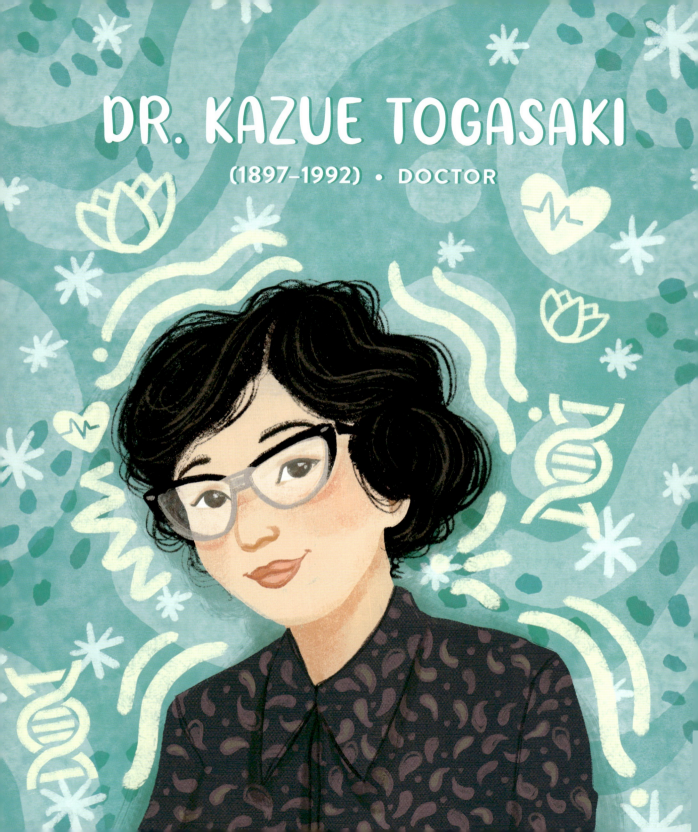

# DR. KAZUE TOGASAKI

## (1897–1992) • DOCTOR

Dr. Kazue Togasaki was one of the first Japanese American women ever to become a doctor in the United States. When she was nine, the 1906 earthquake devasted her community in San Francisco. The young Dr. Togasaki watched her mother turn their local church into a medical center. Helping her mom tend to the wounded inspired her to go into medicine.

After receiving her degree in 1933, Dr. Togasaki opened a very successful practice in her hometown of San Francisco, the heart of the Japanese community, as an obstetrician. She was known for taking in patients even if they couldn't afford medical care, and soon everyone loved and appreciated Dr. Togasaki.

Then, in December 1941, Japan bombed Pearl Harbor. President Franklin D. Roosevelt declared war and marked Japanese people as the enemy, including people living in the United States. Hundreds of thousands of people of Japanese ancestry were placed in internment camps for years, including Dr. Togasaki.

In the camps, Dr. Togasaki did what she always loved doing, which was helping others. She set up a Japanese American team of medical practitioners, most of whom were new graduates and inexperienced. The internment camps weren't built to house any type of medical facility, but they did the best they could with what they had. Being one of the only doctors available, she was moved around from camp to camp, helping her community with their medical needs. One day, Dr. Togasaki had to perform an emergency baby delivery. She ordered the people around her to take down the laundry door so she could use it as a delivery table. She would go on to deliver fifty more babies while detained in these camps.

In 1943, Dr. Togasaki was released from the camp. Just like many Japanese Americans who survived the camps, they returned to their homes and businesses destroyed. She went back to San Francisco and rebuilt her business from the ground up. Dr. Togasaki would serve as her community's obstetrician for forty more years. She provided care, healing, and delivered hope to her patients . . . and over ten thousand babies!

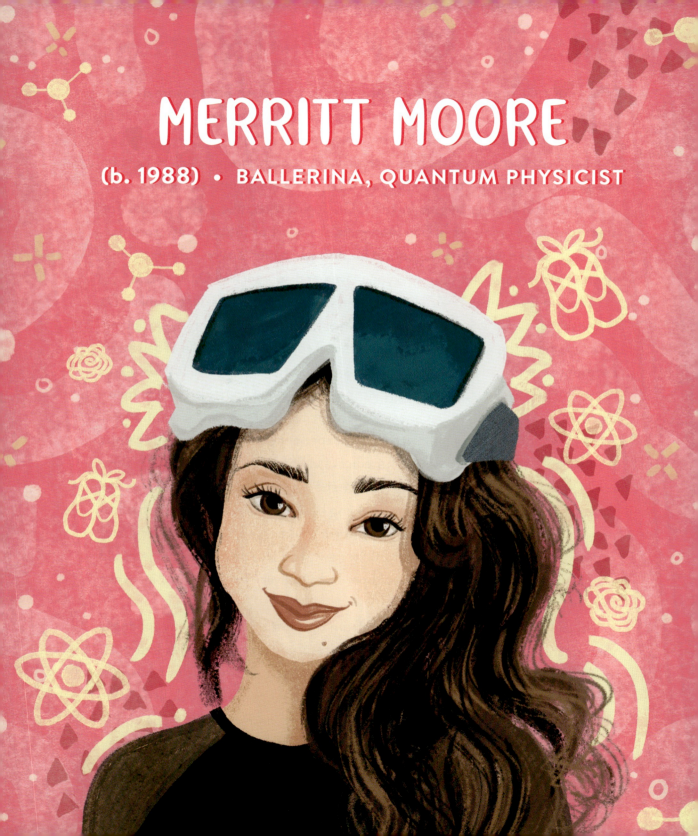

# MERRITT MOORE

(b. 1988)  •  BALLERINA, QUANTUM PHYSICIST

When Merritt and her sister were little, their father would ask questions like "What is dark matter?" and "What do you think infinite galaxies look like?" These questions would run through Merritt's mind and ignite a passion for science. While her excitement for science grew, she also discovered she loved dancing. When Merritt was thirteen, she attended her first ballet class and was immediately hooked. She wanted to be a ballerina. Merritt was a bit behind in training compared to all the other girls, who had started when they were three years old. But that didn't stop her from practicing.

In college, Merritt majored in physics at Harvard *and* joined the Boston Ballet company. It was a rigorous schedule, as she had to juggle both dance rehearsals and lab work. During her second year, with a full class load, she auditioned for ballet companies all around the world and was rejected more than twenty times. For every rejection, Merritt would get back up and try again. Her parents didn't really want her to continue to dance. They saw it as a distraction more than anything. But she wanted to prove she could do both, and she did. Merritt graduated magna cum laude with a degree in physics. She also auditioned for twenty-four major ballet companies around the world. On her twenty-fifth audition, she was accepted into the Ballett Zürich.

Merritt continued her studies at the University of Oxford and earned her PhD in quantum physics all while still dancing as a professional ballerina. During the coronavirus pandemic, shows and events were canceled. While some people chose to take up new hobbies like baking or knitting, Merritt utilized her love of both science and dance and created an industrial robotic arm that would act as her dance partner.

As a professor, artist, and scientist, Merritt aims to redefine human and robot interaction through the arts and encourages younger generations to open their minds to exploring new dance forms. At Harvard, she helped create a robot and human dance duet choreographed by artificial intelligence!

Innovation is her truth, and she leans into that unapologetically.

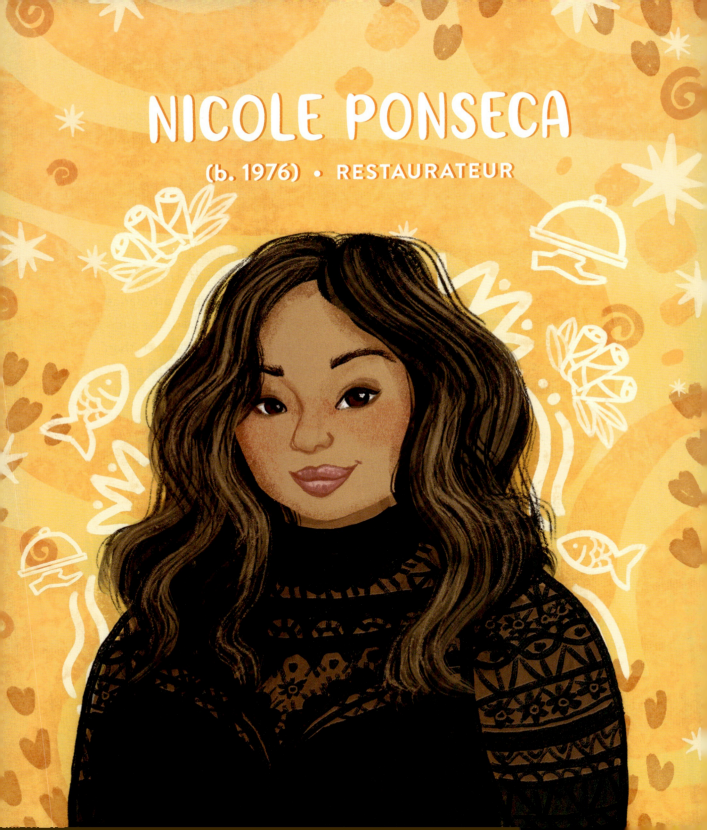

# NICOLE PONSECA

(b. 1976) • RESTAURATEUR

When Nicole moved to New York City, she had $75 and a dream of becoming a successful executive in an advertising firm. Nicole landed an advertising job and was living out her dream, until one day someone asked her where they could find Filipino food. Unlike other Asian cuisines, such as Chinese, Japanese, Korean, and Thai food, very few restaurants served Filipino food. For Nicole, this question would ignite and fuel a desire to come up with an answer. She wanted to open her own restaurant and bring Filipino food to mainstream dining.

She didn't know *how* to open or run a restaurant, so Nicole started from scratch. By day, she would work as an advertising executive, and by night, she would tie her hair back and work as a dishwasher at a restaurant. Nicole did this for years, working multiple jobs as a waitress, hostess, and bartender, learning as much as she could about how to run a restaurant.

Then, in 2011, Nicole had an idea of hosting a small event showcasing all her favorite Filipino dishes. She still didn't have the money to set up her own restaurant, so Nicole asked one of the owners of a place where she worked if she could use their restaurant to hold the event. She called it Maharlika, and it became one of the first pop-up restaurants to ever be created. Maharlika, which was only available on the weekends, started out with a handful of patrons—some of which were Nicole's friends. But after a few rave reviews from a magazine, Maharlika became the place to be, with a three-month reservation wait.

A year later, Nicole opened Jeepney, a restaurant that offered family-style dishes laid out on traditional banana leaves, from which customers were encouraged to eat kamayan-style (with their hands). Both restaurants ran successfully for almost a decade and helped start conversations about Filipino food.

By realizing her dream, Nicole made a seat at the table for Filipino cuisine and for other Asian American businesswomen to eat too.

When Miyoshi was thirteen years old, she was farming rice in Japan; World War II was just beginning. Even with increased tension between Japan and the United States, Miyoshi adored watching American movies. She would admire singers and actors like Bing Crosby gliding across the silver screen, wishing one day she could do the same. One night, some American ships came to dock in her hometown. It was beautiful, she thought, the way the blue, red, and green lights glistened on the water and sky. Miyoshi looked out and enjoyed the view as she listened to the beautiful jazz music on the ships' loudspeakers. From that moment on, she fell in love with jazz music.

A few years after World War II ended, Miyoshi joined a US Army jazz group as a singer. They toured around Japan's nightclubs, and Miyoshi became so popular she caught the attention of a director who was casting for a film in the United States. In 1955, she moved to New York and was cast to play a supporting role in a movie called *Sayonara*, which also starred legendary actor Marlon Brando. The movie was a box office hit. In 1958, it was nominated for many Academy Awards, including Miyoshi Umeki as Best Supporting Actress. She won, making Miyoshi the first Asian American woman to ever win an Academy Award. No other Asian American woman has won this award.

But a lot like the handful of Asian actors to ever make it in Hollywood, Miyoshi was often typecast. She was asked to speak in broken English and play the submissive foreigner. Miyoshi retired from acting in 1972, despite her incredible talent. She was so frustrated with the industry that she was known for etching out her name from the Oscar and throwing her trophy away.

Miyoshi might not have felt seen as accurately as she would have liked in media, but her story is essential to inspiring future actors to reach their full potential. This might be Miyoshi's biggest role of her career.

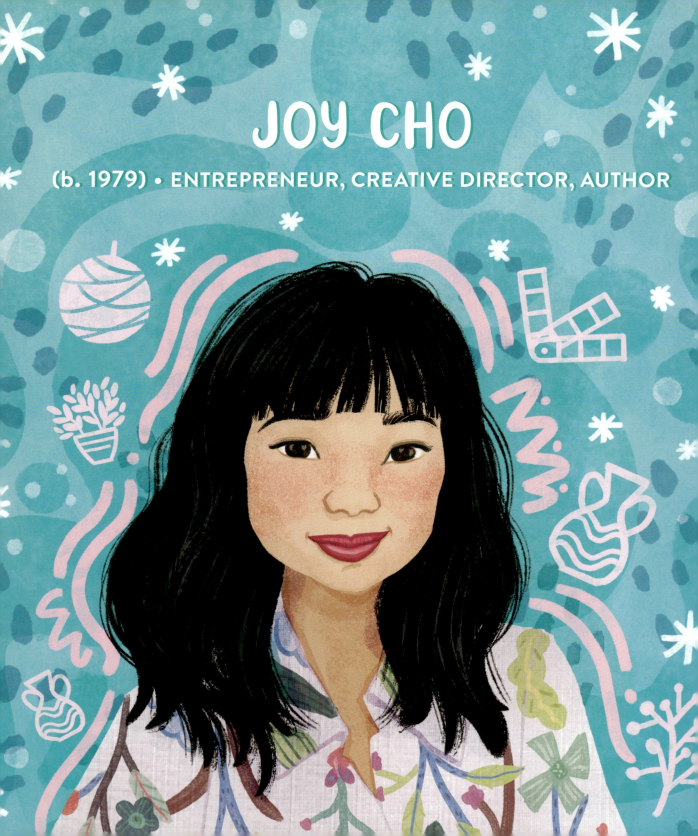

# JOY CHO

(b. 1979) • ENTREPRENEUR, CREATIVE DIRECTOR, AUTHOR

**J**oy is a designer whose philosophy starts off with one simple question: "Does it make you happy?" She combined her love for creating things with her entrepreneurial skills she learned from watching her parents and turned a simple blog into a successful empire.

Joy was born and raised in Philadelphia. Her parents owned a Thai restaurant, where she would spend most of her time trying to entertain herself by crafting things. From a very early age, Joy loved baking, taking care of plants, and creating things like greeting cards for her family and friends. Making things for people made her happy.

Joy's love for crafts evolved into a keen interest in design. After college, she moved to New York and worked as a graphic designer for an advertising agency. It was her years working with clients in the fashion industry that sparked an interest in fashion. When Joy got engaged, she and her future husband decided to move back to Philadelphia. Joy found herself unemployed.

With no prospects, Joy turned to the internet. In 2005, she launched *Oh Joy!* a design blog that documented her life and all her transitions at the time. Joy posted about things she loved and relied on her personal style to shine. Over the next few years, her design blog would gain a large following, allowing more and more clients to find her. She was soon working as a full-time freelance designer.

As a now married woman and a mom of two, Joy's business continues to grow with her. Oh Joy! is a lifestyle brand that creates licensed products and collaborates with major companies such as the Land of Nod (now Crate & Kids), Johnson & Johnson, and Target. In between running her own business and caring for her family, she has written six books. Joy was honored as one of *TIME* magazine's "30 Most Influential People on the Internet" two years in a row, all because she thought to share her happiness with the world.

# DOROTHY TOY

## (1917–2019) • DANCER

Dorothy loved dancing.

When she was a kid, Dorothy's parents owned a restaurant across the street from a vaudeville theater. Dorothy would dance in front of the restaurant for fun. One day, the theater manager saw her and told Dorothy she should take some lessons. Because ballet school was too expensive, her parents enrolled her in a general dance class that was taught by a Russian teacher. Dorothy was a star pupil in class. She was one of the only girls who was able to do some difficult routines of the Russian **Cossack dance**. By taking the general dance class, Dorothy was able to learn all types of moves. She discovered her love for tap dancing and her ability to dance en pointe.

In the 1930s, Dorothy and her sister, Helen, began auditioning for dancing roles in Hollywood films without much success. Paul Wing, a fellow dancer and patron of their family restaurant, suggested they try out for a film called *Happiness Ahead*. The movie was released in 1934 by Warner Bros., and Dorothy, Helen, and Paul were featured performers in the nightclub scene.

The chemistry between Dorothy and Paul onstage was kismet. They formed a duo called Toy and Wing. Even though Dorothy was of Japanese descent, the duo was considered the "Chinese Fred Astaire and Ginger Rogers." Identifying as Chinese during this time was relatively safer than Japanese. Toy and Wing were one of the only successful Asian American duos of the vaudeville era. Known for their combinations of tap, jazz, and even Cossack dancing, they stunned and awed people with their amazing footwork. Toy and Wing performed anywhere and everywhere, from movies to stages and nightclubs. They were even the first Asian American entertainers to ever perform in the Palladium in London. Though World War II negatively impacted their act, Dorothy and Paul would continue dancing together and dazzling audiences years later.

Dorothy broke barriers and paved the way for many Asian American entertainers today. For Dorothy, she was happiest onstage, and the cheers she received was all the reward she ever needed.

# RUBY IBARRA

**(b. 1988) • EMCEE, SCIENTIST, SONGWRITER, DIRECTOR**

Ruby is a bio-tech scientist who works forty hours a week. She does research and runs tests in a lab, helping to find cures for today's health problems. On days off, Ruby is a rapper and spoken-word artist.

Ruby's family immigrated to California from the Philippines in the 1990s. She was only a preschooler when she first fell in love with hip-hop. She loved the way the beat and rhymes made her feel, and hip-hop gave a voice to a younger generation in marginalized communities. It was a movement that Ruby really connected with; it empowered her.

In school, Ruby excelled in science—especially biology. As a daughter of immigrants who found it difficult to find jobs, the importance of education and stability was ingrained in her at an early age. She studied biochemistry and molecular biology in college. After graduating, she became a lab technician at a bio-tech company in San Francisco.

Ruby's first album, *Circa91*, was released in 2017 and gained a massive response. It even earned her a spot on the **Rock the Bells** tour. Ruby raps about her immigrant experience and the challenges of adapting to a new culture while trying to remain true to her roots. Her verses discuss colorism and the lack of representation for people of color in the media. She raps about what she knows. People began to notice how Ruby was using the mic. They saw that she speaks to women, teachers, girls—especially those from the Filipino community. Ruby is giving them a voice.

She also gives back in other ways. Ruby cofounded a scholarship program called Pinays Rising to help Filipina Americans pursuing a college degree. In 2021, Ruby contributed to the research to find a cure for the coronavirus known as COVID-19. In the same year, the San Francisco Immigrant Rights Commission honored Ruby with the Youth Leadership Award for helping inspire immigrant youth in her community.

Ruby's goals are clear. She aims to celebrate her Filipino heritage, help improve society, and inspire the next generation to do the same. And she is just getting started.

# DR. MABEL PING-HUA LEE

(1896–1966) • ECONOMIST, SUFFRAGIST, FEMINIST ACTIVIST

Mabel Ping-Hua was born in Canton, China. During the times of the Chinese Exclusion Act of 1882, Chinese people were denied entry to the United States unless they were considered an important civil servant. Mabel's dad was a missionary pastor, so he was able to move to New York City. Mabel and her mom followed years after, only when she landed a scholarship at a US school. Mabel's parents were pretty progressive for their time and raised Mabel to be a well-educated, independent person.

Mabel's parents also kept themselves up-to-date with feminist politics in both America and China. The **Chinese Revolution of 1911** led to establishing the Republic of China. The women of China made sure that women's rights were included in their constitution. What did all this mean for the ladies? It meant that the Chinese government decided to give women the right to vote.

When the American **suffragists** heard of this news, they were intrigued. They wanted to know how the women in China were able to get their voices heard. The suffragists began welcoming women of Chinese descent to their cause. They invited these women from all across the United States, including Mabel, to speak at their rallies. She was only sixteen years old at the time, but she impressed the heck out of those women by speaking about the racial injustices and prejudices that her fellow Chinese immigrants were dealing with. Even though at that time Mabel wasn't allowed to become a US citizen, she still supported women's rights and equality in hopes that people would all come together to change the nation's views and build a more equal America.

In 1917, because of the work of women like Mabel Ping-Hua Lee, women won the right to vote in the state of New York. Later becoming the first Chinese woman to graduate with a PhD in economics, this fierce feminist helped America take a giant step toward progress.

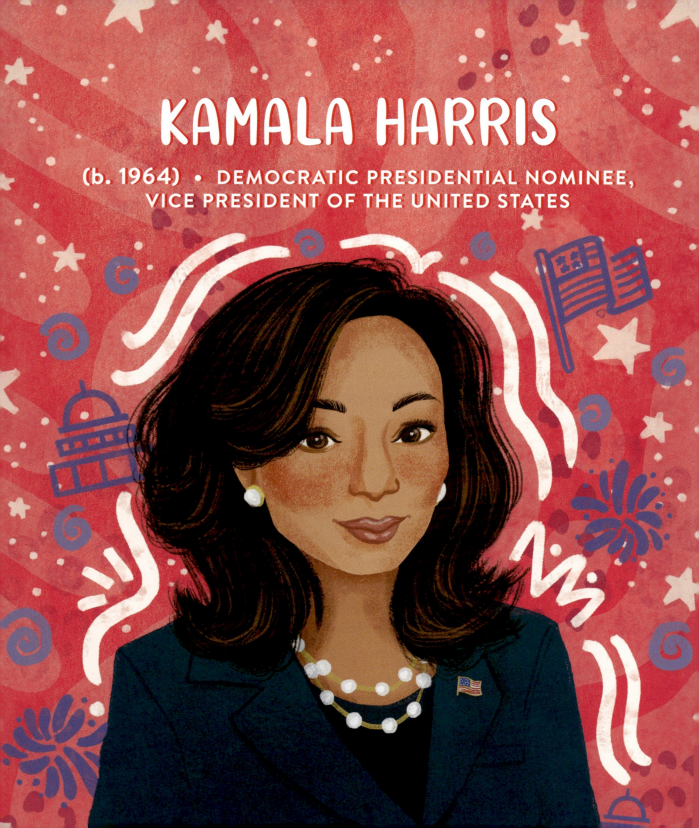

# KAMALA HARRIS

(b. 1964) • DEMOCRATIC PRESIDENTIAL NOMINEE,
VICE PRESIDENT OF THE UNITED STATES

Kamala was born during the civil rights movement. Her dad, Donald, was an economics professor from Jamaica, and her mom, Shyamala, was a cancer research scientist who emigrated from India. Shyamala was determined to raise two confident and socially aware women and surrounded them with strong role models from both cultures of her multiethnic background.

In the 1980s, Kamala majored in political science and economics at Howard University, a historically Black university. In her years at Howard, Kamala became heavily involved in activism and student government.

After earning her law degree and passing the bar in 1990, Kamala worked as deputy district attorney in Alameda County, California. Eight years later, continuing her civil service duties, she became the managing attorney in the San Francisco District Attorney's Office. In 2011, Kamala was elected to be attorney general, making her the first woman and person of color to ever hold this position. In this position, she was also able to implement new ideas to solve her communities' issues, like criminal justice reform and police brutality.

In 2017, Kamala ran for senator of California and won. She was now part of the team that made the changes in our government—and she got right to work. Kamala won settlement cases for families that were affected by the housing crisis, supported the LGBTQ+ community, and used her years of experience as a criminal prosecutor to change California's drug and trafficking policies. Kamala held this position for four years until she ran alongside former President Biden in the presidential race and was elected the forty-ninth vice president of the United States of America in 2021.

Kamala's responsibilities have multiplied since becoming the vice president. Now serving a whole nation and running for president in 2024, her goals remain the same: she wants to make sure her community is safe and taken care of. Vice President Kamala Harris is the first Black and South Asian American woman to ever hold this position. But as she stated in her inaugural speech, she will not be the last. She's counting on the next generation to make that a fact.

# OTHER NOTABLE WOMEN

**Eva Chen**—(b. 1979) Fashion Editor, Journalist

**Joyce Chen**—(1917–1994) Chef, TV Personality, Businesswoman

**Josephine Cheng**—Programmer, Vice President of IBM Research

**Jhené Aiko Efuru Chilombo** (b. 1988)—Musician, Singer

**Cecilia Chung**—(b. 1965) Civil Rights Activist, LGBTQ+ Advocate

**Ann Curry**—(b. 1956) Journalist

**Wilhelmina Kekelaokalaninui Widemann Dowsett**—(1861–1929) Suffragist

**Eileen Gu**—(b. 2003) Olympic Skier

**Mona Haydar**—(b. 1988) Rapper, Musician, Activist

**Mazie Hirono**—(b. 1947) First Female Senator from Hawaii, First Asian American Woman Elected to the US Senate

**Cathy Park Hong**—(b. 1976) Poet, Author, Professor

**Mindy Kaling**—(b. 1979) Actress, Comedian, Writer, Producer

**Christine Sun Kim**—(b. 1980) Sound Artist

**Michelle Kwan**—(b. 1980) Olympic Figure Skater

**Jhumpa Lahiri**—(b. 1967) Poet, Author

**Padma Lakshmi**—(b. 1970) Chef, Author, TV Personality, Philanthropist

**Fei-Fei Li**—(b. 1976) Computer Scientist, Director of AI Laboratory at Stanford

**Lisa Ling**—(b. 1973) Journalist, TV Personality

**Dr. Dawn Mabalon**—(1972–2018) Filipino American Historian

**Natalie Nakase**—(b. 1980) Professional Basketball Coach

**Celeste Ng**—(b. 1980) Author

**Sandra Oh**—(b. 1971) Actress

**Miné Okubo**—(1912–2001) Illustrator, Fine Artist

**Georgina Pazcoguin**—(b. 1984) Ballet Dancer

**Michelle Phan**—(b. 1987) YouTube Influencer, Businesswoman

**Olivia Rodrigo**—(b. 2003) Singer, Actress

**Anna Sui**—(b. 1964) Fashion Designer, Icon

**Toshiko Takaezu**—(1922–2011) Ceramic Artist

**Muna Tseng**—(b. 1953) Dancer, Choreographer, Author

**Jeannette Wing**—(b. 1956) Computer Scientist

**Flossie Wong-Staal**—(b. 1946–2020) Scientist

**Merle Woo**—(b. 1941) Educator, Poet, LGBTQ+ Advocate

# GLOSSARY

**Angel Island Immigration Station**—The Angel Island Immigration Station served as an immigration port between 1910 and 1940 in San Francisco Bay.

**Art Basel**—An annual international art fair that collaborates with the hosting city to assist in growing and enriching art programs. It provides a platform for contemporary artists to show and sell their work to a high-end clientele.

**Black Belt**—Between 1940 and 1960, the homeowners association in Chicago created legally binding contracts that said no existing homeowner could rent or sell their homes to Black people, to keep them from moving into Chicago's white neighborhoods. The "Black Belt" was a row of apartments located on the South Side of Chicago and were the only residential areas that Black people were allowed to live in at the time.

***Brown v. Board of Education of Topeka***—A case taken to the Supreme Court in which a milestone decision was made that ruled against the segregation of public schools based on race.

**California gold rush**—The California gold rush boomed from 1848 to 1855 after gold was found by a carpenter named James Marshall in a river. This led to many people moving to the West Coast in search of gold. It was one of the largest migrations in American history.

**Chinese Exclusion Act of 1882**—An act to institute a ten-year ban on Chinese laborers immigrating to the United States. It prevented people of Chinese descent from becoming American citizens and denied them any citizen rights. This included other ethnicities from Asia and earlier Asian American settlers prior to the establishment of this act.

**Chinese Revolution of 1911**—A successful revolution against the Qing Dynasty, which established the Republic of China, bringing an end to the imperial system.

**Cossack dance**—A Russian folk dance where a person squats low on the ground with their arms folded and kicks their legs in front of them repeatedly to the music.

**Early Childhood Education Act**—Initiated in the 1960s, the Early Childhood Education Act is a variety of laws and programs that provide younger children access to early education so that they're better prepared to enter kindergarten and give them a head start to become successful students.

**EP**—Stands for "extended play." It's a musical recording that contains two tracks or more but not enough to be considered a full album or record.

**Fourteenth Amendment**—An amendment that granted citizenship to all "born or naturalized in the United States."

**haute couture**—*Haute* is French for "elegant" or "high" and *couture* is translated as "sewing" or "dressmaking." Haute couture is the act of creating custom-fitted high-end garments and fashion.

**Japanese American internment camps**—A forced relocation by the US government of thousands of Japanese Americans to isolated detention camps during World War II between 1942 and 1945.

**Junior Olympics program**—A program consisting of multiple levels created to help gymnasts improve their foundation in the sports of gymnastics.

**Khmer Rouge regime**—Dictator Pol Pot and members of the Communist Party of Kampuchea ruled Cambodia from 1974 to 1979 and implemented repressive and violent policies in the country. The regime murdered political opponents resulting in the genocide of an estimated two million people, wiping away nearly 25 percent of Cambodia's population.

**Mars Perseverance rover**—A car-size vehicle launched in July 2020 and used to explore the Jezero crater on Mars as part of NASA's Mars 2020 mission.

The rover successfully landed on Mars in February 2021.

**MasterChef**—An American competitive reality TV cooking show that features amateur and home chefs competing to win the title of "Master Chef."

**Nickelodeon theaters**—A simple theater space, usually set up in storefronts, that projected motion pictures. Popular between 1905 and 1915, the admission fee to watch these motion pictures was a nickel.

**Nineteenth Amendment**—An amendment that granted American women the right to vote.

**Nobel Prize**—An award established in honor of scientist Alfred Nobel and awarded annually to those who have made outstanding contributions to the fields of physics, chemistry, medicine, literature, and peace.

**Partition of India**—Near the end of British rule over the Indian subcontinent in 1947, India was split between two independent states: India and Pakistan. This led to the sudden migration of about fifteen million people to relocate their families because of religious affiliations. It was a very violent and disturbing time in South Asian history, an estimated two million people died, and families are still divided to this day.

**Pearl Harbor**—On December 7, 1941, Japan surprise attacked the US naval base at Pearl Harbor in Hawaii. It destroyed and damaged over three hundred US aircrafts and killed thousands of people. This resulted in the US entry into World War II.

**Reserve Officers' Training Corps (ROTC)**—Reserve Officers' Training Corps is a program offered in colleges across the United States that prepares full-time students to become officers in the US military. Those who join gain access to professional development and scholarship opportunities.

**Rock the Bells**—An annual hip-hop festival concert that features mainstream hip-hop artists and offers smaller stages for up-and-coming new artists.

**suffragist**—A person advocating that the right to vote should be extended to the disenfranchised, especially women.

**Title IX**—A US legislation established in 1972 that prohibits sex-based discrimination in education programs and activities.

**UNICEF**—The United Nations International Children's Emergency Fund was established in 1946 to provide emergency food and health care to children and mothers in disadvantaged communities around the world.

**Women's Educational Equity Act**—An act passed by the US Congress in 1974 that prevents gender discrimination in education. This act provides women equal opportunity for programs, including equivalent federal funding for women's sports programs and activities as men's sports.

**X Games**—A series of sport events mainly held in the United States that showcase athletes with exceptional abilities in skateboarding, BMX, motocross, skiing, and snowboarding.

**yellow face**—The offensive act of wearing makeup to imitate the appearance of an East Asian person, usually worn by white actors.

**yellow slave trade**—In the early nineteenth century, Chinese women and children were imported to America, with the promise of being united with their husbands or fathers. Instead, they were sold as sex workers or indentured servants.

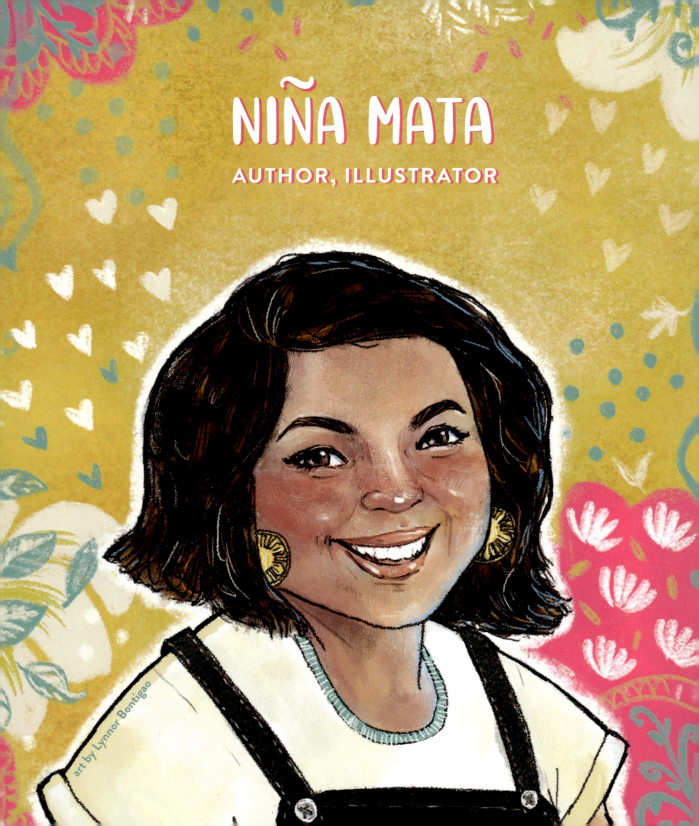

# NIÑA MATA

## AUTHOR, ILLUSTRATOR

art by Lynnor Bontigao

# A LITTLE BIT ABOUT ME:

- I was born in the Philippines and grew up in Woodside, Queens, New York.
- When I was in grade school, I had an irrational fear of mirrors.
- I am fluent in Tagalog.
- I love to sing; karaoke is my favorite pastime.
- I grew up in the New York Public libraries. I've visited them all.
- My favorite book is *Mufaro's Beautiful Daughters* by John Steptoe.
- When I was young, I wanted to be an actress on Broadway.
- My best friend in high school made me join the cheerleading squad. Our squad doubled as a step team. They taught me how to find my rhythm. (Which wasn't easy.)
- When I was a teenager, I wanted to be a DJ. I gave myself the nickname "DJ Skratch 'n' Snip." (That phase lasted one summer.)
- I love all things magic. I always carry crystals with me.
- I love video games. Mostly RPG computer games.
- I don't know how to ride a bike.
- If I wasn't an author-illustrator, I'd probably be a dermatologist.
- I had a dog growing up, and his name was Wiper. His name was actually White Fur, but I couldn't pronounce it.
- I once met a psychic who told me it was imperative that I use my voice. I thought it meant I missed my calling as a performer. But now I'm starting to understand there is more than one way to use one's voice.

Niña Mata is a *New York Times* bestselling illustrator, a NAACP Image Award nominee, and Theodor Seuss Geisel Award honoree. She has illustrated many books, including American gymnast Laurie Hernandez's *She's Got This*, NBA superstar LeBron James's *I Promise*, and the Ty's Travels I Can Read series. Niña currently lives in New Jersey with her husband, their daughter, and Tabitha, their cat. Visit her online at ninamata.com.